for Your Kindergarten Classroom

Photographs: p. 4, 25, 31, 43, 55: James Levin; p. 9: Deborah Feingold.
Illustrations: Rita Lascaro; Cover: Teresa Anderko; pp. 6, 7: Ellen Sasaki.

Printed in the U.S.A.
ISBN 0-590-32773-9

7 8 9 10 3456789/0

Contents

50 Math Activities

Introduction

Math All Around Us

When children have the opportunity to explore materials, they begin to solve everyday problems using mathematical concepts.

It's a typical day in a kindergarten classroom. One child is putting away props in the dramatic-play area by sorting them into boxes. Two other children are standing back-to-back, comparing heights, wondering how much longer until they'll be able to reach the top shelf. Another child announces that tomorrow she'll be five and points to the date on the calendar.

Your classroom is a natural math center, one in which children are exposed to sorting, counting, measuring, and problem solving before they consciously realize that they're actually learning math. When children learn math in real-world situations, they develop the skills needed to communicate and express themselves mathematically, interpret real-world problems and solutions, and validate their thinking. All of these skills will allow children to feel that they have the ability to succeed in mathematics.

Your Role

Children have begun to explore basic mathematical concepts long before they enter the kindergarten classroom. As a teacher, you'll be creating classroom situations in which children have hands-on opportunities for making mathematical discoveries.

- By modeling mathematical language throughout the day, you help children naturally become familiar with mathematical terms in the proper context.
- By creating a mathematical environment in your classroom, you enable children to explore and investigate through open-ended activities, independently as well as collaboratively.

This book offers 50 developmentally appropriate math activities for kindergartners. They are organized by concepts: Grouping and Sorting, Patterns, Numbers and Graphing, Measurement, and Geometry.

As you adapt the activities for your children, keep in mind that they are designed to be open-ended and can be combined with children's ongoing explorations across all areas of the curriculum. Use the Math Setup on the following pages as a guide for gathering materials and equipment to create and enrich your home base for math activities. See how to prepare math grab bags for children's independent exploration on page 8.

Getting the most from the activity plans

The activity plan format is simple and easy to follow. Each plan includes most of the following:

AIM: The purpose of the activity; what children will do and learn.

MATERIALS: Basic math materials and special items to gather. You will find that you have most of these on hand. The rest can be easily donated by parents or local businesses.

IN ADVANCE: Tips for materials to prepare or arrangements to make before introducing the activity.

WARM-UP: Ways to introduce the activity or underlying concept to the group. Open-ended questions help children think critically and probe topics more deeply.

ACTIVITY: Steps and suggestions for introducing materials, helping children get started, and guiding the activity in nondirective ways.

REMEMBER: Social/emotional, cultural, and developmental considerations; tips about ways to relate other skills and concepts to the activity theme; and occasional safety reminders.

OBSERVATIONS: Ideas and strategies for observing children that will help you understand children's individual learning styles as well as help you guide, extend, or evaluate the activity.

SPIN-OFFS: Ideas for extending the activity into different curriculum and skill areas.

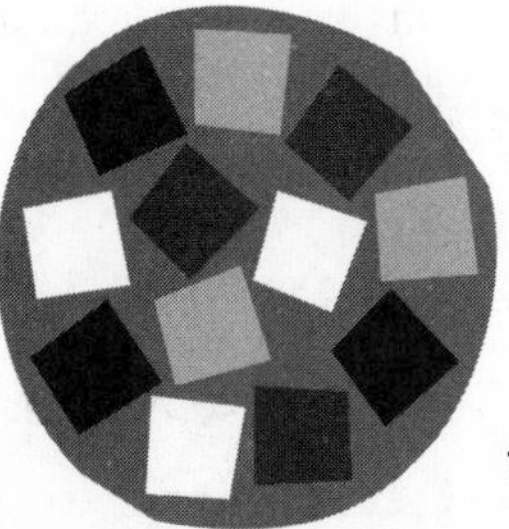

BOOKS: Children's books related to the activity or theme.

Colleagues, aides, student teachers, volunteers, and family members can all benefit from fun suggestions for child-centered math activities. So feel free to duplicate and share the plans for your program's use.

Math Setup

1 Real-world photographs help children discover mathematical concepts in everyday life.

2 A question invites children to use problem-solving and critical-thinking skills as they explore concepts of measurement.

3 Concept books reinforce children's mathematical discoveries about shape, number, measurement, and so on.

4 A display of children's projects encourages the class to examine each other's work and inspires children to communicate about their learning.

5 Forming numerals with different materials (such as pipe cleaners) adds a multisensory dimension to children's mathematical learning.

6 Having counters available (such as an abacus) helps children answer their own counting questions as they arise every day.

7 Number Notebooks allow for cross-curricular learning as children record their problem-solving techniques.

8 Illustrations help children connect symbols with their numerical values.

9 Graphs allow children to use their visual skills in making mathematical comparisons.

10 Children match felt shapes to numerals on a flannel board as they illustrate their ideas about the concept of numbers.

11 A new task card every day invites children to use their problem-solving skills to find solutions to challenging questions.

12 Keeping manipulatives and other materials well organized and accessible to children inspires them to work independently on their own projects.

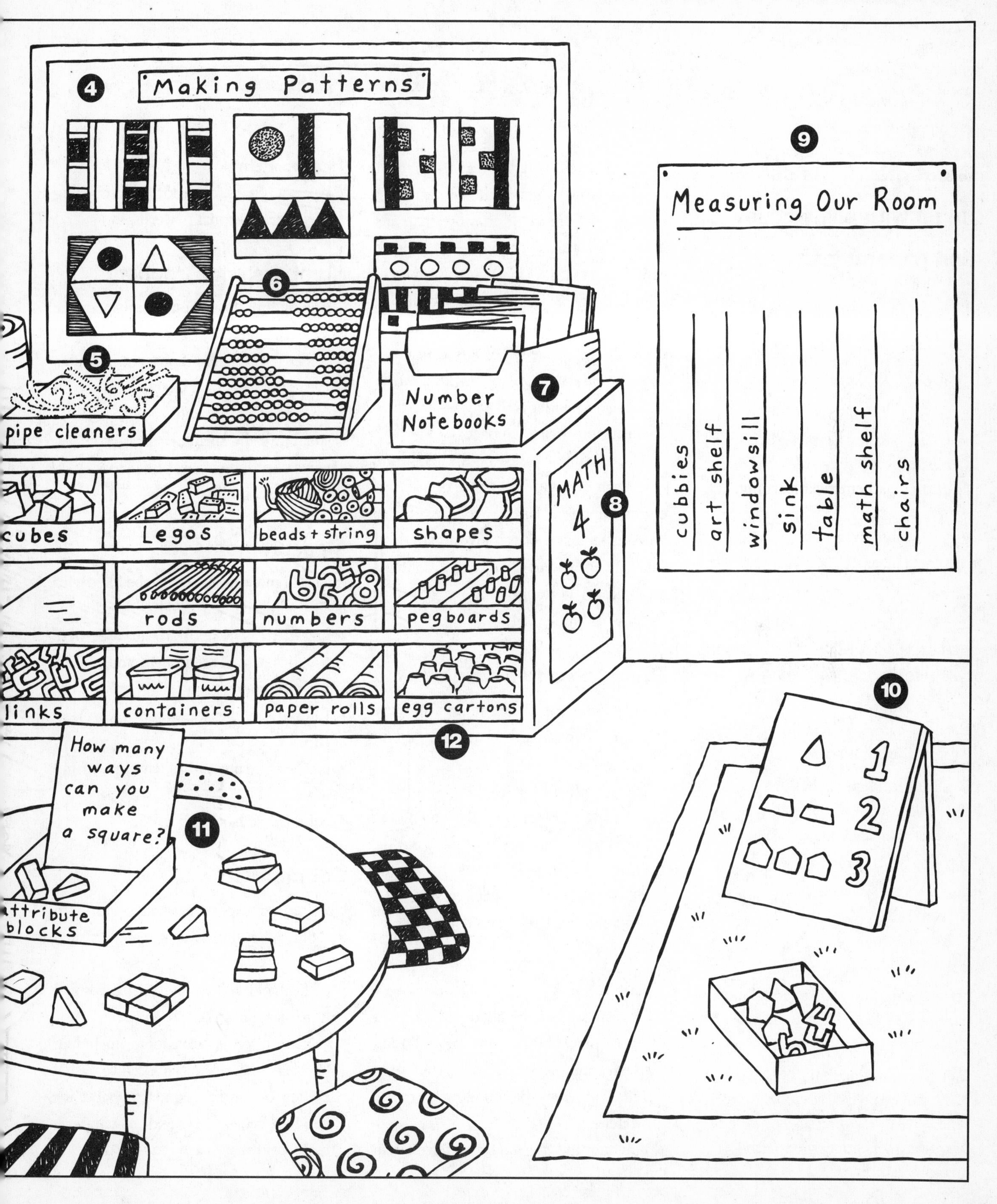

Making Patterns
pipe cleaners
Number Notebooks
MATH 4
cubes
Legos
beads + string
shapes
rods
numbers
pegboards
links
containers
paper rolls
egg cartons
Measuring Our Room
cubbies
art shelf
windowsill
sink
table
math shelf
chairs
How many ways can you make a square?
attribute blocks
1
2
3

Grab a Bag of Math

Great grab bags can begin with pillowcases and paper clips!

Unexpected math learning takes place every day in the kindergarten classroom. To make math more than just a rote, abstract subject, children need to experience math — to see it and touch it.

With grab bags of math, which you can make quickly and easily, children can explore the concepts of *grouping, patterns, numbers, graphing, measurement,* and *geometry* independently — on their own time, at their own pace.

Use old pillowcases for the bags, and label each one with the name of a different concept area. Keep bags accessible to children so that they can investigate them independently, and change the contents periodically. Here are some suggestions for how to fill the bags.

Grouping and Sorting

A wide variety of related items will work best for grouping and sorting. Try filling your bag with:

- lids of different sizes, colors, shapes, and textures, such as jar lids and plastic bottle tops.
- an assortment of dry beans with plastic ice cube trays for sorting.
- different size, shape, and color buttons.

Patterns

This grab bag may be filled with samples of patterns, as well as items for children's own patterning, such as:

- old wallpaper samples and fabric swatches.
- crayons and paper so children can copy patterns.
- pattern blocks for making and copying three-dimensional patterns.

Numbers and Graphing

Graphing can be a concrete experience when children use three-dimensional objects. Make blank graphs and include a variety of objects for children to place on them. You might include:

- small toys and small plastic animals.
- coins of different sizes and colors.
- dried pasta in different shapes.

Measurement

A measurement grab bag can be filled with both traditional and nontraditional measuring devices. Children can use these items to measure themselves and objects around the room. Some suggestions are:

- ruler, tape measure, and measuring cups.
- pieces of string and paper clips strung together.
- cutouts of a hand and a foot.

Geometry

Children can explore geometry with both flat and three dimensional materials such as:

- pictures of buildings and Legos or small blocks for construction.
- a map of your classroom including "buried treasure" for children to find.
- cutouts of various geometric shapes for children to explore and match with real-world shapes around the room.

Activity Plans for Grouping & Sorting

Children are natural observers of the world, and as they grow, so do their powers of observation. They begin to notice details and what makes some things different from others. Teachers can see children's natural grouping and sorting instincts in the classroom every day as they pile blocks, sort food, and make animal families. By guiding them to classify everyday objects, teachers inspire children to explore the foundations of mathematics.

Classifying and categorizing activities help children understand basic mathematical concepts.

Throughout the Day

- During snacktime, serve different types of food. Choose foods with various textures, shapes, sizes, colors, and tastes. Place several empty plates on the table so that children will be encouraged to sort and group their snacks by a variety of attributes.
- Provide a time each day when children can reorganize different areas of the room. For instance, they may choose to sort the dramatic-play area so that all the toys are in one bin and all the clothing in another or so that all the items associated with being a firefighter are together.
- Place an object in an unusual place to see if children notice that it doesn't belong.

Around the Room

- Keep sorting trays and a variety of small manipulatives available so that children can create their own categories for sorting. For example, children may choose to place writing tools and scrap paper in the writing center.
- Encourage children to help organize the materials in the classroom by labeling groups of objects and the places they belong and sorting scissors, pencils, and glue sticks.

Learning Center Sorting

Children will get to know their classroom, area by area.

Materials

- Familiar objects, such as a block, toy car, crayon, scissors, dress-up shoe, shirt, sand sieve, shovel, and various manipulative and puzzle pieces
- photographs of different areas of the room
- cafeteria trays or large sheets of construction paper

Aim

Children will use sorting, classifying, problem-solving, and thinking skills to organize familiar objects around the room.

Warm-Up

Talk about the different areas in your room. Encourage children to tell about the toys and materials found in each one. Ask them if they can find any materials that are used in more than one area. Then, together, make a list of materials that can be used in several areas, such as crayons, pencils, and paper. Beside each item, make tally marks to show the number of areas where the item can be used.

Activity

1 Invite children to name each object and tell something about it—its color, use, where they might find it in the room, and so on. Help children decide specific categories and sort the items according to their categories. You might demonstrate by starting to sort objects by color or size and then encouraging children to finish. Use trays or construction paper as sorting mats to help children focus on the organization of the sorting.

2 Next, ask children to sort the objects according to the areas where they are used. If you provide pictures or drawings of each area, you can use them to mark the sorting piles. Encourage children to talk about why they choose to place the items in the particular areas.

3 Now invite children to collect new items to add to the sorting game. Again, ask them to sort the items in as many different ways as possible. End by sorting the objects according to their areas.

4 At the end of the game, ask children to take the piles to the appropriate areas and put the items away. This helps children become aware of where things go.

Observations

- What attributes do children consider for grouping and/or sorting items into different areas?

Books

Try these books at storytime.

- *The Awful Mess* by Anne Rockwell (Parents Magazine Press)
- *The Big Tidy-Up* by Nora Smaridge (Golden Press)
- *The First Day of School* by Patricia Reif (Western)

SPIN-OFFS

- Extend this activity by putting cleanup words to the tune of "The Farmer in the Dell." You can change the verse to fit the items you are cleaning up.

We're putting our toys away.
We hope it won't take all day.
We have to get done, so let's have fun.
We're putting our toys away.

Animals Everywhere

Children find new ways to look at their favorite toys.

Materials

- stuffed animals
- chart paper
- markers
- glitter
- blue paper
- scissors
- glue

Aim

Children will use sorting, classifying, problem-solving, and comparison skills to graph familiar objects.

In Advance

Send notes home with children asking them to bring in their favorite stuffed animal on a specific day.

Warm-Up

Gather children in a circle with their stuffed animals. Invite each child to introduce his or her stuffed animal to the class. Encourage children to talk about any special or interesting features of their animals.

Activity

1 Have children place their animals in a large group. Invite them to examine the animals closely and point out all the similarities they see among the animals. Record these responses on the experience chart.

2 Then ask children to point out some differences among the animals. Once they begin to see the differences, invite children to sort the animals into groups of their choosing. Use chart paper to make a graph of how children sort the animals.

3 Next, ask children to rearrange the animals to form new groups. On a clean sheet of chart paper, list the new sorting categories and ask children to make tally marks next to the category to which their animal belongs.

4 Then ask children to repeat the activity, forming more groups and graphing their findings. This will enable children to see many of the possible groupings for their animals.

Remember

- Try to keep an extra supply of stuffed animals on hand so that those children who have forgotten to bring in an animal can choose one from the classroom selection.

Observations

- How do children work together to find new categories for their animals?

Books

Share these books about teddy bears.

- *Corduroy* by Don Freeman (Puffin)
- *Paddington Bear* by Michael Bond (HarperCollins)
- *Where's My Teddy?* by Jez Alborough (Candlewick)

SPIN-OFFS

- Ahead of time, use the blue construction paper, markers, scissors, glue, and glitter to make blue ribbons for all of the animals. Have a fun awards ceremony by presenting each child with a blue ribbon for a silly category, such as fluffiest rabbit or most ferocious tiger.

Making Photo Cubes

A closer look at one another leads to new discoveries!

Materials

- colored construction paper
- chart paper
- 1-pint milk cartons
- hand mirror
- photos of children
- markers
- ruler
- glue

Aim

Children will explore their similarities and differences and create graphing cubes to sort and classify what they find.

In Advance

Ask parents to bring in a 1-pint milk carton and a photograph of their child. After receiving these materials, cut off and discard the top of each milk carton. Then divide a sheet of chart paper into columns and boxes to make a large graph.

Warm-Up

Invite children to share ideas about how they are alike and different. Pass around a small mirror so that children can look at and talk about their features.

Activity

1 Invite children to make stackable graphing cubes. Ask each child to completely cover a milk carton with strips of colored paper and to glue his or her photo onto one side of the cube.

2 Ask children to compare their own faces with the faces they see on the other cubes. How are the faces alike and different? Have children work as a group to decide which characteristics to graph, such as hair color or eye color, and label the columns.

3 Show children how they can use the cubes and the large graph to sort, match, and stack the ways they are alike and different.

4 Talk with children about their graphing selections and about how their unique characteristics help make each one of them special.

Remember

- Model descriptive language in a way that positively points out children's unique features.

Observations

- How are children showing an appreciation of one another's differences?

Books

These books celebrate children's differences.

- *Hats Off to Hair!* by Virginia Kroll (Charlesbridge)
- *The Same But Different* by Tessa Dahn (Viking)
- *Why Am I Different?* by Norma Simon (Albert Whitman)

SPIN-OFFS

- Gather children and discuss the words they use to describe themselves. Make a list of the descriptive words on a chart.
- Invite children to place stickers, drawings, or other pictures onto the sides of their cubes for more sorting and stacking activities.

Family Circles

Family here, family there, family everywhere!

Materials

- strands of yarn in different colors
- construction paper
- crayons
- pencils
- markers
- scissors

Aim

Children will create circles and people shapes to show all the members of their family.

In Advance

Draw or trace simple people shapes of different sizes on thick paper. Children can use these shapes for tracing.

Warm-Up

Invite children to talk about the people they live with as well as relatives who live outside their home. Point out that they are all part of one family.

Activity

1 Invite children to draw and cut out people shapes that represent all their family members. Or they can trace or draw faces on the precut people shapes.

2 Help children write their family members' names on the backs of the people shapes and to count the number of people in their families.

3 Invite each child to choose a few pieces of yarn, and help him or her tie the ends of each strand into a knot, creating a circle. Ask children to place the circles of yarn on a table or on the floor, grouping family cutouts who live together. Suggest that they put the cutouts of the people they live with inside of one circle, and the other cutouts inside of the other circle.

4 When they are finished, ask children to describe and compare their circles. They can count the different numbers of people and then move the cutouts around to create different groupings.

Remember

- This activity can help children learn about various family structures.

Observations

- How do children categorize their family members? Do they make up different groupings?

Books

These family books are fun to read!

- *A Birthday for Frances* by Russell Hoban (Harper & Row)
- *If It Weren't for You* by Charlotte Zolotow (Harper & Row)

SPIN-OFFS

- Invite children to use their people shapes in the block area when they build smaller versions of their homes.
- Help children use their family cutouts to make a bar graph.

Play Clay Cookies

Turn play clay into a fun math experience.

Materials

- round cookie cutters
- several cookie sheets
- play clay
- rolling pins

Aim

Children will use fine-motor and math skills as they make and sort circles by size.

In Advance

To make round cookie cutters, save metal or plastic jar tops in several sizes, such as those from pill bottles, small sauce bottles, and large juice bottles. Collect empty thread spools at the same time. Glue a spool to the outside of each cap or lid to create cookie cutters with handles.

Warm-Up

Read a book to your class about the concepts of *big* and *small.* (You may want to choose one from the list below.) Discuss the relativity of these concepts by asking children to name *big* and *small* things. How do their ideas of *big* and *small* compare?

Activity

1 On a low table, put out lots of play clay, rolling pins, and your new round cookie cutters, and invite children to play. As they do, point out the different-sized cookie cutters and the sizes of the circles they make.

2 After children have had time to experiment, bring out a few cookie sheets and put them on the table. Then, sit with children and make a few circles of your own. Place your small circles on one cookie sheet and big circles on the other. As you do, explain how you are sorting the circles by size. Encourage children to join in the sorting.

3 Later, choose three circles of different sizes and arrange them in order in front of you. Show children that you have the circles in order — small, medium, and large. Encourage children to imitate your series.

4 Add to the play clay fun by asking open-ended questions to encourage children's pretend play. Maybe some children are making cookies for a party or preparing special tiny pizzas.

Observations

- How does each child assess his or her understanding of what is big and what is little?

Books

Add these books about big and little to your shelf.

- *Big and Little* by Joe Kaufman (Golden Press)
- *Big and Little, Up and Down* by Ethel Berkeley (Addison-Wesley)
- *Bigger and Smaller* by Robert Froman (Thomas Y. Crowell)

SPIN-OFFS

- Invite children to play a game of "big, bigger, biggest" by asking them to choose a big object, then a bigger object, and finally the biggest object they can find. Do the same with small, smaller, and smallest.
- Invite children to use the cookie cutters to trace circle patterns on paper. Ask children to discuss their patterns with one another.

Shape Search

Dig those shapes!

Materials

- books and magazine articles about bones and dinosaurs
- 5–6 screens, about 12″x12″
- 6–8 small tubs or boxes
- good-sized sandbox
- trowels or small shovels
- chart paper
- white paper
- different-colored chalk
- markers
- smooth pieces of broken pottery

Aim

Children will explore and record unusual shapes as they become amateur archaeologists.

In Advance

Provide children with books and magazine articles on archaeological digs, bones, dinosaurs, and ancient ruins, and allow them to explore.

Warm-Up

Gather children and open a discussion about archaeologists. Talk about dinosaurs and how scientists found their bones in the earth.

Activity

1 Bury in the sandbox all the pieces of pottery you've gathered. Then encourage children to use trowels and shovels to dig carefully for them. Show children how to sift through the dirt with the screens to find small pieces and to brush off their findings gently so they don't get damaged or broken.

2 Invite children to use the chalk to mark their pieces with a number or letter like archaeologists do. Children can keep the pieces they discovered in small boxes or tubs.

3 Ask children to sort the pieces they found according to size, shape, color, or kind. Record results on graph paper, using different columns for each category they created.

4 Ask children to imagine what kind of object their pieces might have come from and why.

Remember

- Before you use the pottery pieces, soak them in a bleach solution to sterilize them, and smooth any rough edges. Try to offer a wide variety of sizes, shapes, and colored pieces to stimulate speculation and discussion.

Observations

- How many ways do children sort and match the pottery? What descriptors do children use to create categories?

Books

These books will dig up more archaeological talk.

- *Big Old Bones* by Carol Carrick (Clarion)
- *Digging Up Dinosaurs* by Aliki (HarperCollins)
- *If You Are a Hunter of Fossils* by Baylor Bird (Macmillan)

SPIN-OFFS

- Take a field trip to a dinosaur museum or to a local area where fossils have been found. (They can show up even in gravel areas in a city!)
- Invite children to create a *Shape Dig* book, drawing pictures of the pieces they found and the objects they might have come from.

Sort, Sort Again

Use everyday objects in different ways.

Materials

- variety of everyday items such as spoons, keys, and lids
- experience chart paper
- markers
- sheets of paper
- trays

Aim

Children will practice flexible thinking as they sort and classify everyday items into a variety of categories.

Warm-Up

Invite children to examine a variety of one type of item, such as keys. Together, brainstorm all the ways that keys can be sorted. Encourage children to look for detailed differences among the keys, such as the number of grooves or the shapes of the holes.

Activity

1 Gather a wide variety of a particular item such as spoons. You may wish to include teaspoons, tablespoons, wooden spoons, measuring spoons, serving spoons, and ice cream scoops. Invite children to examine each item, noticing specific details.

2 Next, encourage children to sort the items in any ways that they choose, such as by size, color, or shape. Provide children with trays or sheets of paper to help them organize their sorting. As they sort their objects, ask children to explain their choices and to label their groups. Encourage children to sort based on a variety of characteristics.

3 Discuss the word *function* with children. Explain that a function is how something is used. Direct children's attention to the objects they are sorting, and explain that these things have a variety of uses. Encourage children to sort and label the items by function.

4 Together with children, make a list of the different ways that the objects were sorted. Provide opportunities for children to share their sorting logic.

Remember

- Sorting by function is more complex than sorting by size or shape because it is based on abstract qualities, not visual ones. Remind children that many items can have more than one function, opening the possibilities for more sorting categories.

Observations

- Do children see more than one function for each item?

Books

These stories show creative ways to use common objects.

- *The Cleanup Surprise* by Christine Loomis (Scholastic)
- *Cloudy With a Chance of Meatballs* by Judi Barrett (Atheneum)
- *The Nightgown of the Sullen Moon* by Nancy Willard (Harcourt Brace Jovanovich)

SPIN-OFFS

- Let children use the collection of items in art projects. For example, they might want to make prints using keys or hang spoons to make a wind chime.
- Encourage children to graph these everyday items, using their sorting categories.

Gobs of Gadgets

Find new uses for everyday items.

Materials

- small gadgets such as switches, screws, washers, coils, and pieces of metal screening
- muffin tins or egg cartons
- markers
- chart paper
- paper bag

Aim

Children will sort and classify gadgets according to a variety of attributes.

In Advance

Ask parents to bring in any gadgets they can find. Check each one for safety.

Warm-Up

Gather children and discuss what a gadget is. Ask children to brainstorm and describe all the gadgets they see in the classroom that are familiar to them. Make a list of these items. Discuss which gadgets children use and how they can use them.

Activity

1 Ask children to brainstorm a list of gadgets found on small appliances or machines. Talk about why these items are important and necessary in order for the machines to operate.

2 Place on a table a "mystery bag" filled with the gadgets. Invite children to shake the bag in order to guess what items might be inside. Suggest that they reach inside the bag to feel the items, too.

3 Empty the contents of the bag onto the table, and ask children to name the items. Encourage them to describe what these gadgets might be used for. Invite children to sort them into muffin tins or egg cartons. Suggest sorting by color first. Then ask them to think of other ways to sort, such as by size, shape, or use.

4 Together, examine the sorted categories. Encourage children to count the gadgets in their separate groups. Then make a graph based on children's observations and classifications.

Observations

- How do children sort the gadgets? What vocabulary words do they use to describe the qualities of the gadgets?

Books

Find more fun ways to use gadgets.

- *Craft Book for Children* by Rosemary Edwards (Word Aflame Press)
- *Crafts From Recyclables* by Colleen Van (Boyds Mills Press)
- *Gizmos and Gadgets* by Phil Baron (Alchemy Communications Group)

SPIN-OFFS

- Provide glue along with cardboard pieces, and invite children to use these items and the gadgets to create unique sculptures. Ask them to make up names and write about their "machines."
- Encourage children to look for other gadgets around school and home. Invite children to keep a running list of gadgets.

Nature Sorting

Go on a nature hunt with a classifying and sorting twist.

Materials

- nature objects, such as leaves, nuts, sticks, and stones
- 1 paper bag per child
- tape or glue
- paper plates
- crayons

Aim

Children will observe, sort, and classify nature materials that they have collected outdoors.

Warm-Up

Collect samples of natural things to share with the children. Then invite all the children to look outside. Gather in a circle, and make a list of the objects that were seen outside. Explain that today the class will be going on a nature hunt to collect all kinds of nature objects. Talk about the kinds of things children can collect, such as leaves, nuts, and twigs, and share your samples. Also talk about things they shouldn't collect, like leaves and flowers that are still growing.

Activity

1 Give children small paper bags to put their objects in. If possible, divide children into groups of three or four, with an adult accompanying each group. Then bring everyone outside, and let the nature search begin.

2 As they collect their nature objects, ask children to identify them and guess where they might have come from.

3 Have children bring their paper bags inside, and invite them to sort and classify their items. Ask each group how their natural objects are the same and how are they different.

4 Invite children to place their sorted objects into piles on different paper plates. Help them name the categories they are using. Sorting categories might include type of item, shape, size, color, and texture.

Remember

- Be sure to stress the importance of preserving objects in nature — for example, not picking a blooming flower and not touching eggs in a bird's nest.

Observations

- What unusual and imaginative ways do children have for grouping their items?

Books

Here are some books about the kinds of changes autumn brings outdoors.

- *Autumn* by Richard Allington and Kathleen Krull (Raintree Publishers)
- *Fall Is Here!* by Jane B. Moncure (Children's Press)
- *What Happens in the Autumn?* by Suzanne Venino (National Geographic)

SPIN-OFFS

- Invite children to graph how many of each object have been collected. Prepare a large graph with your children, using a marker or crayon to divide the paper into vertical columns, one for each type of nature object. Divide these columns into one-inch square boxes. Leave room at the bottom of each column so children can attach the appropriate object to that spot. Demonstrate how to color one box for each item counted.

A Group Grocery Store

The best way to learn math concepts is from real-life experiences.

Materials

- empty boxes, cans, and other food containers
- grocery-store sales circulars
- experience-chart paper
- play money
- stick-on notes
- markers

Aim

Children will use the mathematical skills of sorting and classifying, counting, and matching numerals to items.

In Advance

Send a letter home to families requesting that they save empty food containers and grocery-store sale circulars. Check local food stores for promotional cardboard food-display shelves that are no longer needed.

Warm-Up

Gather your group to talk about grocery stores. Together, create a list of items a grocery store sells. Brainstorm a list of materials they would need to operate a grocery store, and decide how they might get these things.

Activity

1 Discuss where and how children want to set up a store in your setting and what they will do to organize it. Record their ideas on experience-chart paper. Best of all, research the project together with a visit to a local grocery.

2 Once children bring in their collections of food containers, they can begin organizing the store by sorting and classifying foods. Ask children to create their own ways to sort—by type of food, meals, size, color, or shape of container. Encourage children to try sorting in a variety of ways.

3 Distribute stick-on notes for marking prices. Children can invent prices for items or "read" them in sales circulars, writing them in their own ways on the notes. Provide simple play money for making purchases.

4 Together, think of the other ways to use and extend your grocery store. Some children may enjoy making shopping lists with the sale circulars. Others may want to organize a special sale on selected items or create advertisements.

Observations

- Do children use counting skills in the exchange of play money?

Books

Share these books at storytime.

- *The First Book of Supermarkets* by Jeanne Bendick (Franklin Watts)
- *General Store* by Rachel Field (Little, Brown)
- *Little Bear's Pancake Party* by Janice (Lothrop, Lee & Shepard)

SPIN-OFFS

- Give children a specific amount of play money, and send them on a shopping spree to buy as many different items as they can for that amount of money.
- Give children coupons, or invite them to make their own. Ask children to use their coupons as they shop and see how much money they can save.

Mail Call

Find a useful purpose for your junk mail.

Materials

- collection of junk mail
- boxes
- paper
- markers
- experience-chart paper

Aim

Children will use critical-thinking skills as they develop many simple and complex ways to sort and classify junk mail.

In Advance

A few weeks before this activity, begin collecting junk mail. You may wish to write a note home to parents requesting that they also gather junk mail for this activity.

Warm-Up

Begin a discussion about the post office with children. Encourage them brainstorm different types of mail and how they think the mail is organized before it is delivered.

Activity

1 Show children your collection of junk mail. Together, brainstorm a list of ways to sort the mail. Suggest categories such as size of envelopes or types of stamps. Write the list on experience-chart paper.

2 Next, invite children to examine the mail carefully and then sort it into categories of their choosing. Provide boxes for the different categories. Children may wish to make labels for the mail.

3 Choose several children to act as postal workers. Have them gather a few pieces of mail from each box to deliver to the remaining children in the class.

4 Encourage each child to sort and classify the mail that he or she received from the postal worker. Ask children to see how many different ways they can sort their mail. Repeat this activity until all children have had a chance to deliver the mail.

Remember

- Remind children not to open any envelopes, as this may detract from the purpose of the activity. Set aside another time for children to open the mail.

Observations

- Are children able to pick out subtle details for sorting, such as designs on stamps or numbers in addresses?

Books

These stories show creative ways to use common objects.

- *Postal Workers A to Z* by Jean Johnson (Walker LB)
- *The Post Office book: Mail and How It Moves* by Gail Gibbons (Harper)

SPIN-OFFS

- Invite children to write letters to their classmates and design and color envelopes, using the junk mail as a model. Next, have them decorate a shoe box to use as a mail box in their cubby or desk. Encourage children to send mail to each other and to sort the mail as they choose.

Create a Texture Book

Children explore their sense of touch by classifying textures.

Materials

- different-textured materials (such as cotton balls, velvet, aluminum foil, straw, paper, burlap, and dried leaves)
- large sheets of oaktag or construction paper
- glue
- crayons
- scissors
- stapler

Aim

Children will use observation, classification, and language skills while exploring objects with different textures.

Warm-Up

Let children touch and explore the objects freely for a while. Then talk about the different textures. Encourage children to feel the objects again. Help them find words to tell about each other by modeling descriptive language: "Look, this one feels bumpy. Can you find another one that is bumpy?" Allow plenty of time for everyone to touch and comment.

Activity

1 Children will naturally begin to find objects that have the same texture (two furry objects, for example, or two rough objects). Ask them to group the like-textured items together. As they work, discuss the items, talking about children's methods of grouping them. How are the grouped items alike?

2 Some children may want to be "texture scientists." Give each child an item to hold and examine, and then suggest that he or she search the room for another object that feels the same. The process of matching similar textures helps children practice comparative thinking.

3 Together, sort the textured scraps into similar piles. Then, after providing oaktag and glue, invite children to choose a pile and make a collage. Use each collage as a page, collating and stapling the pages into a group texture book.

4 Review the book together, asking children to describe and compare the textures. Invite children to dictate captions describing their pictures.

Observations

- Are children able to group textures in more than one category, such as "soft and bumpy"?

Books

Share these books to help children understand more about texture.

- *Find Out by Touching* by Paul Showers (Thomas Y. Crowell)
- *My Bunny Feels Soft* by Charlotte Steiner (Alfred A. Knopf)
- *Pat the Bunny* by Dorothy Kunhardt (Golden Press)

SPIN-OFFS

- Extend the activity by creating a "texture cube." Invite children to paste texture scraps on the sides of a large cardboard box. Ask them to group materials so that one side has all rough objects, another all smooth, and so on. Then store the cube in your quiet corner. Feeling its textures can be a calming experience.

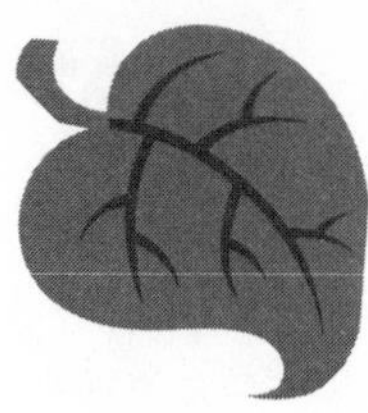

Leave It to Me!

Children make new discoveries by taking a closer look.

Materials

- plastic bags
- paper plates or pans
- leaves
- magnifying glasses
- chart paper
- marker

Aim

Children will observe, classify, and compare different types of leaves.

Warm-Up

This is a good activity for autumn, when children notice the bright colors of the changing leaves. Children who are unfamiliar with fall foliage may benefit from seeing photographs. Ask children to share their ideas about collecting leaves; will they collect fallen leaves or take leaves right off the tree?

Activity

1 During playground time, have small groups of children take turns collecting leaves. Have each child take leaves from at least three different trees in the playground or school yard. Encourage children to use magnifiers to observe similarities and differences even among leaves from the same tree. Then ask them to place the leaves in plastic bags.

2 Set up a leaf-sorting center in your math area. Gather magnifying glasses and plates or pans for sorting. Encourage children to consider characteristics such as size, color, and shape while they sort.

3 Invite small groups to be leaf detectives who examine and compare the different types of leaves. Encourage children to talk about the different colors, smells, and textures.

4 Record children's observations and discoveries on an experience chart. Ask children if they think all leaves are alike and which leaves are their favorites.

Remember

- Pick leaves only from trees with which you are familiar. Watch out for poison ivy!

Observations

- What leaf characteristics do children consider while sorting them?

Books

Share these books about trees and leaves.

- *Have You Seen Trees?* by Joanne Oppenheim (Addison-Wesley)
- *Song of the Seasons* by Robert Welber (Pantheon)
- *A Tree Is Nice* by Janice M. Udry (Harper & Row)

SPIN-OFFS

- Use construction paper and paste for children to create a leaf collage. Invite children to collect more leaves and paste them to construction paper. Encourage them to make leaf patterns or other imaginative designs. Leaf rubbings may also be included. Then bind the pages together to make a class leaf book. Children may also want to dictate captions for their pages.

Mathematical Snack

What could be more fun than an edible sorting activity?

Materials

- large mixing bowl
- shelled peanuts
- 2 varieties of low-sugar cereal
- 4 small mixing bowls
- 1 paper plate per child
- raisins

Aim

Children will enjoy sorting, classifying, and graphing ingredients for a healthy snack.

In Advance

Place the separate bowls filled with peanuts, raisins, and cereals on a table. Ask children to wash their hands to prepare for this activity.

Warm-Up

Let your children know that they will be preparing an energizing treat made up of healthy ingredients.

Activity

1 Invite children to examine the ingredients. Then mix all the ingredients together in a large bowl, and invite each child to place a handful onto his or her plate.

2 Ask children to sort their snack into separate piles. Suggest as categories item, size, color, and shape. As they eat, ask children how they sorted their snack. Encourage them to explain their reasoning by using words such as *round*, *square*, *big*, and *small*.

3 When they finish, invite children to take second servings. Ask them to sort it and line up their piles into rows from bottom to top. Encourage children to look at these simple "bar graphs" to compare the amounts of each ingredient.

4 Ask for suggestions about ways they can change the amounts in each column. For example, they might want to make all the columns even. Or they might make "steps" by putting one item in one column, two in the next, and so on. This way, children can practice the math concepts of "more and less" and counting. After the graphing, enjoy eating your healthy snack!

Observations

- In what ways do children use the bar graph to draw conclusions about "more and less"?

Books

These books are good resources for tasty recipes to make with children.

- *Concept Cookery* by Kathy Faggella (First Teacher)
- *Learning Through Cooking* by Nancy J. Ferreira (Redleaf Press)
- *Super Snacks* by Jean Warren (Gryphon House)

SPIN-OFFS

- Encourage children to sort and classify other objects in the classroom, such as blocks, dramatic-play items, and toys.
- After snack or lunchtime, have children create a graph about what they had to eat, such as peanut butter sandwiches or carrot sticks. Invite children to draw conclusions about their classmates' likes and dislikes.

Friendship Soup

Everyone can feel special when you make "group soup."

Materials

- 1 vegetable from each child
- canned or powdered soup stock
- crackers
- several plastic serrated knives and vegetable peelers
- 1 cup per person
- 1 plastic spoon per person
- soup pot
- hot plate or stove
- long wooden spoon
- ladle

Aim

Children will have an opportunity to sort and measure as they contribute to a group cooking project.

In Advance

Send a note to families asking them to contribute a fresh vegetable that their child likes. As the vegetables arrive, label them with children's names.

Warm-Up

Invite children to show their vegetables and to talk about the different odors, shapes, and sizes.

Activity

1 Ask children to help fill the soup pot with stock. Explain that you will need enough to make 1/2 cup for each person.

2 Help children wash, peel, and cut the vegetables. Then put the pieces in the pot. Be sure to demonstrate the safe way to use plastic knives and peelers.

3 When all the vegetables are in the stock, place the pot on a hot plate or stove. Bring the liquid to a boil. Then simmer for one hour or until the vegetables are soft. As the soup cooks, invite children to notice the changes in texture, color, and aroma. Supervise carefully as you help children use a wooden spoon to stir the soup.

4 While the soup is cooking, ask children to set the table by placing cups, spoons, napkins, and crackers out for each person. Then serve the soup as a warm, tasty snack.

Remember

- Consider boiling root vegetables — beets, potatoes, carrots, and so on — ahead of time to make cutting easier.

Observations

- What characteristics do children use to sort their vegetables?

Books

Read these books about friends and sharing.

- *Best Friends* by Myra Berry Brown (Golden Gate)
- *George and Martha* by James Marshall (Houghton Mifflin)
- *The Great Flower Pie* by Andrea Di Nota (Bradbury Press)

SPIN-OFFS

- Set out a basketful of vegetables (real or pretend), and invite children to "harvest" them by sorting them into groups. Then gather children to discuss the various groups they make. You may also invite two or three children to devise a way to share the vegetables. How can they make the portions even?

Activity Plans for Patterns

Patterns surround children every day in many ways: on floor tiles, wallpaper, even windowpanes! Noticing regularity or the lack of it is a way for children to sharpen their observational skills and gain understanding of relationships. Through repeated experience with activities that invite them to identify and reproduce patterns, children begin to understand basic mathematical concepts. Soon children are able to extend the patterns they see and create their own!

Through identifying and creating patterns, children learn about regularity and predictability.

Throughout the Day

- Keep a running list of where children see patterns in the course of their day. Children will love describing the patterns they found on the sidewalk on their way to school, patterns formed by the desk arrangement in the classroom, and patterns made by the repetition of words in their favorite books.

- Allow time for children to make predictions about patterns — to predict what comes next. Children will enjoy filling in the last line of a repeating story or trying to line themselves up boy, girl, boy, girl when they go outside for playtime.

Around the Room

- Make a "fabric-swatch bin" containing fabric samples with regular patterns and random designs. Invite children to identify fabrics with patterns. Encourage them to express what makes the pattern.

- Introduce the concept of *symmetry* by making masking-tape lines down the middle of objects in the room. Does the object look the same on each side? Why or why not?

Copycat Patterns

Children will have fun matching shapes together.

Materials

- attribute blocks or parquetry tiles
- plastic placemats or trays

Aim

Children will practice matching and patterning shapes as they play cooperatively.

Warm-Up

Over time, offer children opportunities to recreate patterns in many curriculum areas by playing copycat games. For example, string four beads in a pattern, and invite children to do the same. Or, ask one child to build a block design, and encourage others to copy it. You could also invite children to use markers or colored pencils to create simple patterns on graph paper and then have them recreate the designs using cut-out squares. Other repetition activities might include songs where children repeat what you sing or a silent game of "Simon Says," where children copy your movements or the movements of others.

Activity

1 Introduce one of the copycat games to children. Then, when they are familiar with it, encourage them to play together in pairs. Begin the patterning activity by showing the colorful shapes and plastic trays to a small group. Invite children to talk about and play with the shapes.

2 Choose three shapes, and place them in a pattern on the tray. Hand each child an empty tray, and invite him or her to choose the appropriate shapes to re-create your pattern.

3 Play the game again, this time adding more shapes to your pattern if children seem ready for a greater challenge. Encourage one child to make an original pattern and another to copy it.

4 Together, place the trays and shapes in your math or manipulative area for use during independent play.

Remember

- This is only one of many ways to use attribute blocks and parquetry tiles. Encourage children to play the copycat game, but be flexible if they choose to use the materials in other ways.

Observations

- Are children able to identify different names of shapes as they make their patterns?

Books

Look for these books about shapes and patterns.

- *Fire Engine Shapes* by Bruce McMillan (Lothrop)
- *Hide and Seek* by Keith Baker (Harcourt Brace Jovanovich)
- *Shapes* by Fiona Pragoff (Doubleday)

SPIN-OFFS

- Invite children to sit in a circle. Choose one child to be the "guesser," and ask him or her to leave the group. Then choose one child to be the "pattern leader." This child will use hand motions (claps, snaps, taps) to create a pattern and change the pattern every few minutes. Children in the circle copy the pattern leader. Invite the "guesser" to sit in the center of the circle and guess who is leading the pattern.

Patterns Are Everywhere!

Children will create their own patterning chants.

Materials

- collections of a variety of objects such as buttons, bottle caps, pencils, pictures or stickers of animals
- chalk

Aim

Children will notice and create patterns with objects, pictures, hand-clapping, and words.

Warm-Up

This activity is designed to help children see, hear, and say patterns. Start talking about this by using a few objects to make a simple, repetitive pattern: for example, bottle cap/button, bottle cap/button. Ask children to "read" the pattern they see. Then ask them what comes next in the pattern. Together, say the pattern a few times as a chant.

Activity

1 Once children feel comfortable reading and chanting patterns, move on to helping them create their own. A simple pattern like bottle cap/button/bottle cap is called an ABA pattern because each element is repeated once, one after the other. Help children understand this concept by using different objects to make ABA patterns together.

2 Ask children to choose two different objects, such as toy cars and pencils, to make their ABA patterns and encourage them to chant their patterns with you.

3 Next, introduce movements to go along with the chanting by taking one of the ABA patterns and helping children choose a movement to go with each element in the pattern. For instance, you might clap when you chant "bottle cap" and pat your knees when you chant "button." Now you are creating patterns that everyone can see, hear, and experience.

4 Look around the room for ABA patterns on the walls, windows, and people's clothes. Then chant them together. Children may start chanting patterns they make with blocks, manipulatives, their snacks, and even themselves!

Remember

- Anything with a rhythm can be a pattern. Be open to children's creativity for finding and creating patterns in music, movement, and language.

Observations

- Can children find patterns in unfamiliar objects as well as in familiar objects?

Books And Records

Enjoy these books and records about patterns.

- *The Dot and the Line* by Norton Juster (Random House)
- *Edward and the Boxes* by Dorothy Marino (Lippincott)
- "Copy Cat," from the record *Kidding Around With Greg and Steve* (Youngheart Records)

SPIN-OFFS

- Gather children outside and ask them to create a pattern hopscotch game. Invite children to draw various geometric shapes to form a pattern that they can jump and hop through.
- Heighten children's awareness of language patterns by reading predictable or rhyming books. Invite children to point out word patterns and predict text.

Moving Patterns

Here's a simple movement activity to do again and again.

Materials

- drum
- rhythm sticks
- 2 spoons and 2 forks or 2 crayons and 2 pieces of paper

Aim

Children will practice patterning while they use gross-motor, listening, and direction-following skills.

Warm-Up

Put out a few items in an obvious pattern: crayon/paper, crayon/paper or spoon/fork, spoon/fork. Then, using a rhythmic voice, point to each item in order, and name it. Invite children to clap along and name the items. Help children notice that they can see the pattern with their eyes, feel the pattern with their hands, and hear the pattern with their ears. Allow plenty of time for children to experience different patterns by using their eyes, hands, and ears.

Activity

1 Invite children to join you in a large open area for a movement activity and ask if anyone can think of a way to make a pattern using their whole body. Demonstrate a few movement patterns such as step/step/jump, step/step/jump or hop/hop/step, hop/hop/step.

2 Encourage children to say and clap the pattern as you make the movements. Then invite children to move in the pattern with you. You might use a drum to beat the pattern as everyone moves.

3 Next, ask if anyone would like to make up new movements to your drum pattern. Suggest that everyone sit while one child moves in a pattern to the beat of a drum: beat/beat/pause, beat/beat/pause.

4 Encourage others to help by saying the movements aloud and clapping. As you beat the drum, for example, the child might clap, clap, then sit while everyone chants "clap-clap-sit, clap-clap-sit." Repeat this step until all children have had a chance to make up movements to the drum pattern.

Remember

- Keep patterns simple at first. Children can make them more complex as they become accustomed to the activity.

Observations

- Are children able to create patterns by doing the same movements again and again?

Books

Enjoy these music and movement stories together.

- *The Old Banjo* by Dennis Haselry (Macmillan)
- *Something Special for Me* by Vera B. Williams (Greenwillow Books)
- *The Troll Music* by Anita Lobel (Harper & Row)

SPIN-OFFS

- Form a pattern by taping shapes to the floor. Invite children, one at a time, to follow the pattern as you help them say the name of each shape. For example, your "pattern path" might be circle/square, circle/square. Repeat it as many times as space allows.

Mitten Math

Pairs of mittens or socks make natural math materials!

Materials

- 8–12 pairs of mittens or socks in various sizes and colors
- 2 baskets
- thin rope
- clothespins

Aim

Children will use matching, patterning, and small-motor skills as they arrange mittens on a clothesline.

In Advance

Ask families to send in pairs of old mittens and/or go to tag sales or used-clothing stores to buy inexpensive pairs of mittens. When you have enough, put one mitten from each pair into a basket and the corresponding mittens into another basket. Place both baskets in your dramatic-play area. In the same area, hang as a clothesline a long piece of thin rope at children's eye level. Put a pile of clothespins nearby.

Warm-Up

Leave the baskets of mittens, clothesline, and clothespins in your dramatic-play area. Observe how children use them in their play.

Activity

1 Gather with a few children in your dramatic-play area. Take a few mittens from one basket, and hang them on the clothesline in a pattern such as blue/red, blue/red or solid/striped, solid/striped. Talk with children about the pattern you made.

2 Now invite two children to work together to copy your pattern, using the corresponding mittens from the other basket.

3 Next, let children take the lead. Encourage one or two children to choose mittens and hang them on the clothesline in an interesting pattern. This time, you match the pattern they make.

4 As children begin to understand the game, they can work in pairs to create and match one another's mitten patterns.

Observations

- How do children articulate the mitten patterns they have created?

Books

Check these teacher-resource books for more hands-on math ideas.

- *Hands-On Math* by Janet Stone (Scott, Foresman and Company)
- *Workjobs* by Mary Baratta-Lorton (Addison-Wesley)
- *Workjobs II* by Mary Baratta-Lorton (Addison-Wesley)

SPIN-OFFS

- You can use the mittens for further math play. Over time, suggest games such as sorting mittens by color shades, categorizing them by size, or ordering them from small to large. Use the mittens as concrete objects for counting. Invite children to think of other ways to use the mittens. Encourage them to experiment and enjoy.
- Add socks and hats to the clothes basket for more complex patternings.

Patterning With Blocks

Help children practice patterning with a new twist!

Materials

- unit, table, or colored blocks
- patterned cloth swatches
- patterned clothing, such as sweaters or scarves
- floor tiles with patterns
- wallpaper samples with patterns

Aim

Children will identify, describe, and create patterns using blocks.

Warm-Up

Show children objects that have recognizable patterns, such as a striped scarf, checkered material, a wallpaper sample, and so on. Discuss the patterns together. Point out the ways they repeat themselves. Encourage children to look at each other's clothes to see if anyone is wearing a repeating pattern. Now play a simple people-pattern game to help children experience the concept. First make a boy/girl, boy/girl pattern. Invite a few children to line up in front of the group, and ask the others to say the boy/girl pattern aloud. Ask, "What would come next in the pattern — a boy or a girl?" Have children continue to add to the pattern. Try another people pattern such as stand/sit, stand/sit. With each pattern, encourage children to say or chant it, and ask, "What comes next?"

Activity

1 Have children try to create patterns with blocks. Show children a simple two-block pattern such as square/triangle, square/triangle. Encourage children to continue the pattern.

2 Next, try three-part patterns. This time, ask children to choose three different shapes or colored blocks and create their own patterns. Help them see that the same order of colors or shapes should be repeated over and over.

3 Encourage children to say, chant, or sing their patterns as they build them. This auditory clue helps children incorporate the pattern concept.

4 If children are ready for a challenge, have them create a pattern wall with blocks. Show them how a pattern can be built into one long, continuous wall. When the walls are complete, have children describe their patterns to the group.

Observations

- Do children use patterning language, such as triangle/square, triangle/square, as they build?

Books

Here are some good books for observing patterns around us.

- *Changes, Changes* by Pat Hutchins (Macmillan)
- *Look Again* by Tana Hoban (Macmillan)
- *Zoo City* by Stephen Lewis (Greenwillow Books)

SPIN-OFFS

- Point out incidental patterns that children create as they work with materials such as pegs, beads, and interlocking plastic blocks. Take walks to look for patterns inside and outdoors.
- Older children may enjoy making patterns for each other to copy. Photographs of child-made patterns can be displayed where children can see them as they play.

Activity Plans for Numbers & Graphing

Children have a natural fascination with numbers. Just think of how many times you've heard your children debate who has more of a certain object, then finally decide to settle it by counting the objects.

As children's counting skills become more advanced, they love to answer the question "How many?" Comparison also plays a key role as they explore the concepts of *more* and *less*. Graphs provide a concrete visual representation through which children can deepen their understanding of these concepts.

Throughout the Day

- Give each child a unit block with his or her name on it. Post a "Question of the Day" ("Do you like peanut butter?" for example), and invite children to place their blocks in the "yes" or "no" stack. A different three-dimensional graph can be discussed each day!

- Elicit children's help when situations arise that require counting or numbering. Children will naturally enjoy helping out the teacher by counting out the papers (one per child) or preparing for snacks.

Around the Room

- Collect counting books with different themes to keep in your class library. Invite children to compare the different ways numbers are represented in each book.

- Hang up graphs you've created with children. Post a sheet with the question "What does this graph tell you?" below each one. Invite children to write or dictate their observations.

Through graphing activities, children learn to visually represent the concept of numbers.

Singing Number Songs

Help children discover the musicality of math.

Materials

- experience-chart paper
- colorful markers
- toys and other props
- magazines
- glue
- child-sized scissors (optional)

Aim

Children will find the rhythm in counting by singing and chanting number songs.

In Advance

Use experience-chart paper to write the lyrics to some popular counting songs like "Five Little Monkeys" or "This Old Man."

Activity

1 Bring experience-chart paper to group time. Explain that today you're going to sing some counting songs, or songs with numbers. Show children one of the counting songs, and read it aloud. Then sing the song together! Encourage children to clap or tap out rhythms, in addition to using their voices.

2 When you finish, ask children to suggest another song. Then write it down, and sing together. Repeat this process until you've listed a few songs. Next, invite children to illustrate the chart using markers or pictures they cut from magazines. Save your chart to refer to whenever children want to sing a number song.

3 Because counting aloud can be too abstract to be meaningful for young children, encourage your group to use hand motions or fingerplays that show "how many." You can also use toys or props as characters in the songs — for example, five stuffed animals to represent "Five Little Monkeys."

4 As you sing, ask children to adjust the numbers accordingly as the verses change.

Remember

- Number songs give children an opportunity to play with the "language" of math. Hands-on experiences with manipulatives help children to understand the concrete meaning of that language.

Observations

- In what ways do children use manipulatives to aid them in counting?

Books

Count along with these books.

- *One Light, One Sun* by Raffi (Crown)
- *Ten, Nine, Eight* by Molly Bang (Scholastic)
- *This Old Man* by Carol Jones (Creative Edge Publishers)

SPIN-OFFS

- Use children's favorite songs to act out number stories. Children will enjoy being "added" or "subtracted" according to the verse. At the same time, they'll experience counting with their whole bodies.
- Invite children to make up their own number "songs," counting parts of their bodies or objects in the classroom.

Look How We're Alike!

Children will match and compare to find out about themselves.

Materials

- flash cards of various colors
- large sheets of construction paper
- markers, crayons, or paints

Aim

Children will practice matching and one-to-one correspondence skills.

Warm-Up

Invite children to sing and move to the tune of "If You're Happy and You Know It." Use descriptive words such as "If you're (five or a girl or a boy) and you know it, shake your (head or clap your hands or stomp your feet." After each verse, stop and ask questions such as "Who's five? Did everyone shake their head the same way?" Continue with each verse.

Activity

1 Hold up colored flash cards one at a time and ask children with matching hair color to stand up. Observe to see if everyone who is supposed to be standing is standing. Continue holding up cards and asking questions about eye, shirt, pants, dress, skirt, and shoe color.

2 Then call out specific combinations of attributes such as "all children with brown hair and blue shirts," and ask children to stand when they hear a combination that pertains to them. Continue to call out attributes until the entire class is standing.

3 Next, place children in pairs and invite them to point out the similarities between themselves and their partners. Encourage them to look beyond characteristics of color and to notice characteristics such as hair length and texture.

4 Finally, invite children to create self-portraits on large sheets of construction paper. Encourage them to use paints or crayons to match their own hair, eye, skin, and clothing colors.

Remember

- Help children to comment on one another's attributes in a positive way. Model language that is descriptive and nonjudgmental.

Observations

- Do children recognize their own attributes accurately?

Books

Here are books filled with pictures to match and pattern.

- *The Button Bow* by Margarette S. Reid (E. P. Dutton)
- *Ten Little Mice* by Joyce Dunbar (Harcourt Brace Jovanovich)
- *When One Cat Woke Up* by Judy Astley (Dial Books)

SPIN-OFFS

- Gather children together, and explain that you have a secret theme they must guess. For example, your theme might be "children who are wearing stripes." Call out the names of children wearing stripes, and have them stand. Ask the other children to guess your theme. Once children are familiar with the game, they may enjoy making themes of their own.

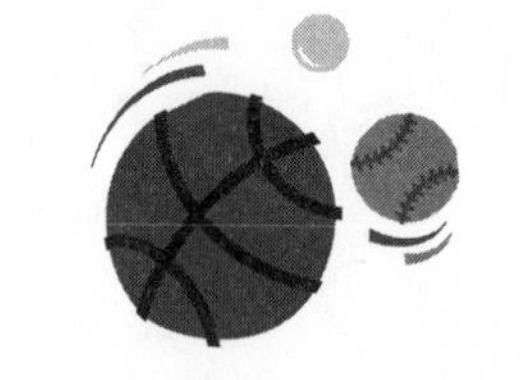

How Big Is Biggest?

Children find out through hands-on experience.

Materials

- small ball, block, apple, or orange
- bag or pillowcase filled with objects, each just a little bigger than the other

Aim

Children will use the math skills of comparison, serialization, and enumeration, along with observation, language, and group-interaction skills.

Warm-Up

Talk about the concept of *big*. Invite children to brainstorm a list of all the things they think are big, and go over the list together. Ask if items are all the same size or if some are bigger than others. Ask children which item they think is the biggest of all.

Activity

1 Gather a few children together to do a big-bigger-biggest activity. Show them the ball (or other object) that you have brought in, and then place it on the left-hand edge of a table. (This helps children practice left to right progression.) Invite a child to find something in the bag that is a little bigger than the object you brought in, and ask them to place it on the table next to the ball. Together, compare the size and decide whether or not it is just a little bigger.

2 Next, ask another child to look for something just a little bigger than the second object and place it next to the others for comparison. Continue until all the objects in the bag are out and you have created a line of objects that increase in size across the table.

3 Now, look around the room together for things that are just a little bigger still. Eventually, your line may have to go off the table and continue onto the floor or another table. By the end of the game, the biggest thing in line may be a child — or even you!

4 While the children are playing, make a point to stress the words *big*, *bigger*, and *biggest*. Help them see that as the line gets longer, things that were considered bigger or even biggest are no longer so.

Observations

- What factors do children use to determine what makes one item bigger than the one before? Length? Width? Volume? Weight?

Books

Share these books about size.

- *Big and Little* by Joe Kaufman (Golden Books)
- *Bigger and Smaller* by Robert Froman (Thomas Crowell)
- *Blue Sea* by Robert Kalan (Greenwillow Books)

SPIN-OFFS

- This activity may also be done in the opposite direction, going from biggest to smallest. Start with a medium-sized object on the left-hand edge of the table, and look for something that is just a little smaller. Continue from left to right until children find something teeny-tiny for the end, such as drawing a little dot for the smallest thing.

Matchmaker

Bead bracelets are fun to make and match!

Materials

- tape
- colored markers
- 10 3″ x 5″ index cards
- 20 10″ pieces of string
- 3′x 3′ pegboard with about 10 hooks
- large wooden stringing beads

Aim

Children will develop one-to-one correspondence as they match beads to bracelets.

In Advance

Draw a straight line (to represent a piece of string) on each index card. Next, draw or trace four, five, or six beads of various shapes on each line and put the cards aside. Then wrap tape around one end of string (for easier threading) and tie a knot in the other end.

Activity

1 Invite children to explore the beads and strings. Suggest that they string beads with the colors and shapes they like.

2 Next, put the beads and strings out on a table with the index cards. Invite children to look at the shapes of the beads and the shapes on the cards, and ask them to try to string their beads in the same order to make a bracelet. Then ask them to choose the markers that match the colors of the beads on their bracelets. Help them color the index-card beads to match the beads on the bracelet they have made. Tape each card under a peg on the pegboard, and put bracelets in a basket.

3 Bring the completed pegboard and the bracelets to circle time. Stand or lean the board next to you, within children's reach. Then place the basket of bead bracelets on the floor in front of the board. Invite children to choose a bracelet, and help them name the colors they see.

4 Encourage children to find the same bracelet on an index card and hang it on the hook above that card. Repeat until all the bracelets are hanging. Now place the pegboard and basket of bracelets in your math or manipulatives area for children to use independently.

Observations

- Are children able to match the circular bracelets to the linear pattern cards?

Books

Share these books about shape and form.

- *A Kiss Is Round* by Blossom Budney (Lothrop, Lee & Shepard)
- *Shapes, Shapes, Shapes* by Tana Hoban (Greenwillow Books)
- *The Wing on a Flea* by Ed Emberley (Little, Brown)

SPIN-OFFS

- Many young children are beginning to count. They might enjoy the challenge of using all the same beads on a bracelet and matching their bracelet on an index card that has the same number of beads.

Sidewalk Number Line

What can children do with objects they find?

Materials

- blocks
- props from your block area
- large pieces of colored chalk
- 10 buckets
- objects children find outdoors

Aim

Children will develop beginning number concepts as they place found objects on a group-constructed number line.

Warm-Up

Gather two groups of children in the block area. Ask one child in the first group to select one block, another child to select two blocks, another to select three blocks, and so on. Then ask children in the second group to do the same, selecting numbers of block-area props (trucks, animals, and so on) instead of blocks. Now ask everyone to find his or her partner — the child who has the same number of blocks or props.

Activity

1 Invite children outside to collect natural objects, such as rocks, leaves, and twigs.

2 Discuss and compare the items. Then encourage children to sort them into the buckets to see how many of each type they found.

3 Next, turn the sidewalk into a number line. Have children work as a group to count 10 pavement squares, or ask children to make 10 large squares using chalk. Number the squares 1 through 10. Now ask children to look at the sorted natural objects and decide which objects can go into which squares. For example, they might choose to put one rock in the first square, two leaves in the second, three twigs in the third, and so on.

4 When the number line is completed, encourage children to "read" it from beginning to end: "one rock, two leaves, three twigs," and so on.

Remember

- Number line activities are a great way to help children make the transition from rote counting to rational counting using one-to-one correspondence.

Observations

- Listen for children's use of comparison and counting terms such as *how many*, *more*, *less*, and *the same*.

Books

Add these counting books to your library area.

- *How Many, How Many, How Many* by Rick Walton (Distributed by Gryphon House)
- *One Smiling Grandma* by Ann Marie Linden (distributed by Gryphon House)
- *Who Wants One?* by Mary Serfozo (Scholastic)

SPIN-OFFS

- Invite children to use the number line in games they invent. To help them start, you might ask, "Can you use the number line to play hopscotch?" Children can jump inside the boxes and do the indicated number of movements they choose, like hops, snaps, claps, or winks. Another kind of game is "singing" the number line by using the items as words in counting songs such as "This Old Man."

Playground Math

Benches, swings, slides, trees — have fun counting these!

Materials

- dots or circle stickers in 4 colors
- large sheet of oaktag paper
- clear adhesive paper
- permanent black marker
- clear tape

Aim

Children will use one-to-one correspondence to count items.

Warm-Up

Draw four columns on the oaktag, and apply the clear adhesive on top. Bring the laminated oaktag and stickers outside. Ask children to name four items they see at the playground and record one in each column (for example a slide, swings, trees, and sand buckets). Invite children to draw a picture next to each of the words.

Activity

1 Encourage children to predict how many of each playground item there are. Then decide which item to count first.

2 Use a different-colored sticker to count the items in each category. As children find the items they chose to count first — trees, for example — invite them to place one sticker for each tree in the tree column. Then search for the item in the next column, using a different-colored sticker. Continue until children have found and recorded every item in all four categories on the oaktag chart.

3 Hold up the oaktag, and encourage children to use the stickers to help them count the items in each column of the chart.

4 Remind children what item each color sticker stands for, and then invite them to make comparisons. Are there more trees or more swings? More shovels or more trees?

Remember

- Try to make sure that the stickers are spaced evenly in each column so that children can easily see "more" and "less."

Observations

- Are children able to make the symbolic connection between the stickers and the actual items they represent?

Books

Here are some fun counting books to share.

- *Count and See* by Tana Hoban (Macmillan)
- *My Red Umbrella* by Robert Bright (William Morrow & Co.)
- *Over in the Meadow* by Ezra Jack Keats (Four Winds Press)

SPIN-OFFS

- Make a larger graph, with a column for each child in your class. You may want to count the number of members in children's families or how many books each child reads in a given week. If you cover the graph with clear adhesive and using wipe-off markers, you can use it over and over again for different topics.

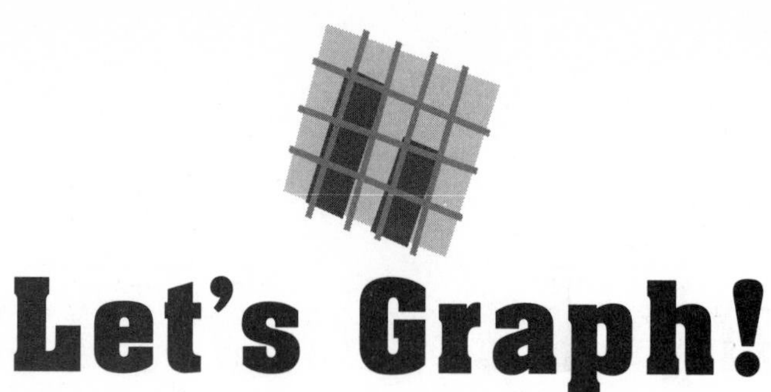

Let's Graph!

Children can make graphs as they sort familiar objects.

Materials

- markers
- ruler
- sets of objects such as cars, planes, and blocks of different shapes and sizes
- large sheet of easel or mural paper
- clear contact paper

Aim

Children will classify and compare classroom objects in this large-scale graphing activity.

In Advance

To make a large graph, use a ruler to divide the easel or mural paper into columns. Then divide the columns into boxes that are big enough to fit the actual items you plan to graph. Cover the graph with clear contact paper, so you can use it over and over again.

Warm-Up

Put out a set of objects, and encourage children to discuss their similarities and differences. Suggest different ways to sort the objects, perhaps by color, size, or function. Together, classify all the objects until they are sorted into piles.

Activity

1 Ask children which pile they think has the most items in it. Explain that they will be using a graph to find out.

2 Ask a child to take one object from the first pile and place it in a box in the first column of the graph. Continue to place items from this pile into the boxes in the first column until all the items are on the graph.

3 Move on to the second pile, and invite children to place these items into the second column. If there are more than two piles, continue until everything has been graphed.

4 Now encourage children to observe the columns. Ask them which one they think has the most objects. Invite children to check their guess by counting objects.

Remember

- Use objects that are smaller than the boxes on your graph so that children can clearly see the graphing lines.

Observations

- How do children use the graph to make comparisons?

Books

These books have pictures of items that children can classify and sort.

- *Cars and Trucks* by Michael E. Goodman (Western)
- *A Child's First Picture Dictionary* by Lillian Moore (Putnam Publishing Group)
- *Clothes* by Ann Morris (Ideals Publishing)

SPIN-OFFS

- During a cooking activity, children can graph the items they will use. Encourage them to think about specific ways to sort — for instance, by food and nonfood.
- The graph can also be used to vote on classroom issues such as which snack the children would like to have on a particular day.

Vehicle Graphing

Put children in the driver's seat with this activity.

Materials

- graph paper (1″ squares)
- watch or timer.
- plain white paper
- crayons
- magazine pictures of different types of vehicles
- trays (to rest tally sheets on)

Aim

Children will observe, count, and graph neighborhood vehicles.

In Advance

Help children make tally sheets, one for each type of vehicle you can expect to find in your area and at least one for a vehicle that is fairly uncommon. Paste the appropriate magazine picture at the top of each tally sheet.

Warm-Up

Share photographs and illustrations of a variety of vehicles, and discuss with children the different types. Ask them how each vehicle is used and where they may have seen it.

Activity

1 During an outdoor activity time, invite a group of children to observe the vehicles that go by. Ask them what kind of vehicle goes by the most.

2 Choose a safe observation spot and ask children to pick a particular vehicle to watch for. Show them how to make one line, or tally mark, each time they see their vehicle go by. Set a watch (or timer) for a minute or two, and start your watch!

3 When the time is up, help children count the number of marks on their sheets. Collect all of the data and make a graph together by drawing or pasting a picture of each of the tallied vehicles at the bottom of the graph paper.

4 Ask children to color the same number of boxes as the number of cars, buses, or trucks. Then ask children which type of vehicle went by the most and which went by the least.

Remember

- If your play area is near a heavy traffic zone, it may be necessary to group children in pairs. One child can count traffic while the other child tallies it.

Observations

- What methods do children use to accurately tally the number of vehicles they see?

Books

These books illustrate different types of vehicles.

- *ABC of Cars and Trucks* by Anne Alexander (Doubleday)
- *Big Red Bus* by Ethel and Leonard Kessler (Doubleday)

SPIN-OFFS

- Try doing this activity at different times of the day or on different days. Save your graphs and compare them. Ask children to think of questions and situations for their graphs, such as finding out what times of the day the most cars go by. They may then think of still other questions and situations for graphing.

Picture Cubes

Create three-dimensional graphs together!

Materials

- 1-pint milk cartons (1 per child)
- liquid detergent
- photo or drawing of each child.
- clear tape or self-adhesive vinyl paper
- tempera paint
- paintbrushes
- white paper

Aim

Children will make picture cubes and use them to graph, predict, estimate, and count.

In Advance

Cut the top off the milk cartons to form cubes. Then cut the white paper into squares slightly smaller than the bottom of the milk cartons. Finally, just before you're ready to begin, mix some detergent into the tempera to thicken the paint.

Warm-Up

Show everyone how to use thickened tempera to paint the cubes. When the cubes are dry, help children attach their pictures onto the bottom of the cubes using clear tape or clear contact paper.

Activity

1 Make a simple drawing to represent a boy and another to represent a girl. Place the drawings on the table or the floor. Then ask children to place their cubes in the appropriate category.

2 Use this graph to determine if there are more boys or girls in the class. Then ask children to think of other things they can graph by using the cubes, such as eye color, hair color, and types of shoes.

3 Ask children to choose between two books at story-time. Place the two books on a table, and encourage children to place their cubes in a column next to the book they would like to hear.

4 Ask children to identify the book that most of them want to hear. Children might also vote on snack choices, rules, names for pets, and games to play outside.

Remember

- Keep it visual! It is essential to have a drawing, photograph, or the actual items on the table when children are making the graphing towers or columns.

Observations

- In what ways do children stack their cubes so they can easily count their results?

Books

Here are books that deal with math concepts.

- *Boxes! Boxes!* by Leonard E. Fisher (Viking Kestral)
- *How Far Is Far?* by Alfred Tresselt (Parents Magazine Press)

SPIN-OFFS

- Use the cubes for prediction and estimation activities. Try a ramp-and-balls game. Have children place their cubes at the spot where they think the ball will stop rolling, or ask children to predict tomorrow's weather by placing their cubes in the column that represents a specific weather picture.

Create A Group Salad Bar

Make a salad and learn about graphing, too!

Materials

- several plastic serrated knives
- plastic forks for each child
- experience-chart paper
- pictures of salad ingredients
- plastic bowls for serving
- bread
- variety of salad ingredients (children bring in from home)
- paper plates
- oil and vinegar
- markers
- butter
- toaster

Aim

Children will use the mathematical skills of counting, comparing, grouping, and graphing as they graph salad ingredients.

In Advance

Use a large sheet of chart or graph paper to make a salad-bar graph. Make columns of boxes that can be colored in. Be sure the boxes are the same size, so the bar graph readily shows "how many."

Warm-Up

Ask children if they have ever been to a salad bar. "What kinds of foods are there? If we were to make a salad bar, what foods do you think we should serve in it?" List the foods children suggest, and invite volunteers to each draw one food under a column on the chart. Then ask children to each bring in one vegetable from home.

Activity

1 When children arrive with their vegetables, invite them to look for the column representing their ingredient and color in one square for each item they brought.

2 Help each child wash and prepare (peel, cut, grate) his or her own ingredient. Together, place the prepared ingredients on paper plates, and arrange them on a low table. A small group of children can make salad dressing while others toast and butter bread for croutons.

3 Encourage children to line up, serve themselves the ingredients they choose, and make their own personal salads. Now dig in!

4 Discuss the graph and emphasize the comparative math concepts of *most*, *least*, and *same*. Together, think of questions that can be answered with your graph.

Observations

- How do children use comparative language while preparing their salad bar?

Books

Try these cookbooks for more cooking and graphing ideas.

- *Crickets' Cookery* by Pauline Watson (Random House)
- *Easy Cooking: Simple Recipes for Beginning Cooks* by Ann Beebe (William Morrow & Co.)
- *Kids Cooking Without a Stove* by Aileen Paul (Doubleday)

SPIN-OFFS

- Invite children to make individual recipe cards for their salads. Encourage them to list their ingredients by drawing or scribble-writing. Organize these recipes in a class recipe-file box.

Make Your Own Snack Mix

Children use their sense of taste to create a new treat.

Materials

- variety of snack foods (such as small crackers, cheese, pretzels, cereal, grapes, raisins, popcorn)
- several small sheets of paper for circles
- large paper cups and napkins
- large chart paper
- tape
- strips of paper
- markers
- paper plates
- a few pencils

Aim

Children will compare tastes and use creative problem-solving skills as they make their own snacks.

In Advance

Prepare a taste-test graph. List children's names down the left-hand side of the large paper, marking a row across the sheet for each name. Across the bottom of the paper, tape a sample of each food item. Mark off a column for graphing above each item. Cut paper circles and draw smile faces on them.

Activity

1 Invite children to put each of the foods on a separate paper plate. Have them take a piece from the first plate and talk about how it tastes. Ask how they would describe it. "Is it sweet? Sour? Salty? Smooth? Crunchy?" Encourage children to use as many descriptive words as possible.

2 After they've had an opportunity to taste each of the ingredients, ask them to choose two favorites. Give them two smile faces each to cast their votes on the graph.

3 Interpret the graph together. Ask children what the graph tells us about likes and dislikes in the class. How could this graph be helpful?

4 Next, offer each child a cup to create a snack mix by combining their two favorite tastes with other tastes. As you eat, talk about the ingredients children included in their "recipes." Encourage them to compare their creations with others.

Remember

- Have fun with the food combinations children would not like to taste. Consider exclaiming "Yuck!" loudly as a group — this allows children to voice their feelings without getting carried away.

Observations

- Notice whether children are conforming to the group or independently voicing their own taste likes and dislikes.

Books

Here are a few books that explore the world of taste.

- *Everybody Has a House and Everybody Eats* by Mary McBurney Green (Addison-Wesley)
- *Miss Pennypuffer's Taste Collection* by Louise B. Scott (McGraw-Hill)

SPIN-OFFS

- For the next week or so, ask children to keep a list of all the foods they eat, including breakfast, lunch, snacks, and dinner the night before. At the end of each day, graph these foods. At the end of each week, invite children to determine which foods were the most popular that week.

Activity Plans for Measurement

As children grow and change, they notice the ever-growing and changing world around them. Whether it's planting a flower and watching it bloom, watching a clock while waiting for an exciting event, or measuring the passage of time season by season, children will become aware of the many different ways in which things can be measured.

Children especially love measuring their own bodies to keep track of their growth. Cooking is another popular activity in which measurement plays a key role. Whether they are using a tape measure, a teaspoon, or the length of their own feet, children build a strong mathematical foundation through measurement activities.

Measuring is a hands-on way to explore numerical value.

Throughout the Day

- Set out a variety of timers at various centers, and during free play, invite children to explore and experiment with them.
- Organize your day so that children will be able to anticipate which activities or events come first, next, and last in their daily routines.
- Expose children to a variety of measuring devices in a natural way, such as by placing measuring cups and spoons in the cooking area, setting up a pan-balance scale in the science area, or keeping string, blocks, rulers, and graphs in the math area.

Around the Room

- Keep a weekly and monthly calendar in a prominent spot so that children can mark off days or become familiar with the sequence of months in a year.
- Put up a growth chart at the beginning of the year, and measure each child. Do periodic checks so that children will be able to see how much they're growing.

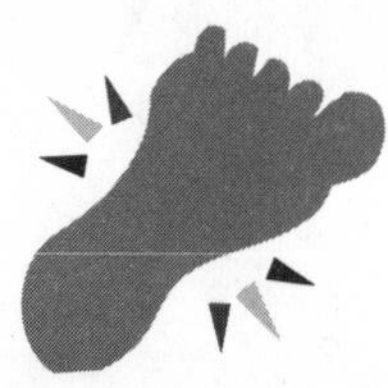

"Me" Measuring

Children will begin to see how big they really are.

Materials

- experience-chart paper
- construction paper
- markers
- crayons
- scissors

Aim

Children will make observations and estimations and use comparative-language and thinking skills in using their bodies as a unit of measure.

In Advance

Take off your shoes and trace your foot on a sheet of paper. Cut out your tracing.

Warm-Up

Show children your foot picture. Explain that you are going to use the foot to measure things. Ask children to estimate which items in the room they think are about the same size as your foot. Let each child use the cutout to test his or her guesses. Next, find things that are bigger or smaller than your foot. Ask, "What can you find that is about two of my feet long?"

Activity

1 Help each child trace their own hand and foot on a sheet of construction paper and then cut out the pictures.

2 Invite children to compare hand and foot cutouts with one another. Ask children to discuss such things as which ones are longer and which ones are wider. Invite children to compare their cutouts to yours to determine which is bigger.

3 Ask children to estimate together what items in the room they think are about the same size as their foot. Record their ideas on an experience chart.

4 Next, encourage children to check out their predictions using their cutouts. Try other estimations. What objects are about two or three hands long? Can they build something out of blocks that is about two hands long?

Remember

- Some children may be anxious to guess a "correct" answer. Remind them that the purpose of the activity is to practice their guessing skills, which will improve with time.

Observations

- In what ways do children use their cutouts to measure objects? Do children use a combination of hand and foot cutouts to measure things?

Books

Here are some good books about children and growing.

- *The Growing Story* by Ruth Krauss (Harper & Row)
- *Peter's Chair* by Ezra Jack Keats (Harper & Row)
- *Where I Begin* by Sarah Abbott (Coward)

SPIN-OFFS

- Use adding-machine tape or ribbon to measure children's heights. Encourage them to take their "Me Strips" around the room to measure objects that are the same size, bigger, or smaller. Save the strips for end-of-the-year comparisons.
- Invite children to use their strips to measure favorite things in the classroom. They can then compare their height with that of the items they chose.

As Big as Me!

Ready, get set, measure!

Materials

- adding-machine tape
- yarn
- wide ribbon
- scissors

Aim

Children will practice measuring, observing, and comparing.

Warm-Up

Discuss with children the different ways they have grown this year and the kinds of growing changes they have noticed. If you took measurements at the beginning of the year, compare them to children's measurements now. Encourage children to bring in clothes or shoes that are now too small for them to wear and compare them to their present sizes.

Activity

1 Gather children outside on a sunny day and ask them to think about what else grows like them. Look for signs of growth in plants and trees in your area. (New growth appears as the lighter green area on the ends of branches and plants.)

2 Use pieces of yarn to measure how much the plants have grown. Ask children to look for the plant that has the most new growth on it.

3 Separate children into pairs. Ask one child in each pair to lie down on a clean area, and invite the other child to measure his or her length using a strip of ribbon or the adding-machine tape. Help cut the ribbon or tape to the appropriate length. Then invite children to switch roles. Invite children to look around for objects that are the same size they are. Ask partners to help each other hold the lengths of ribbon or tape to test out their guesses and measure objects that might be their size.

4 Afterward, children can look for things that they think are bigger or smaller than they are. At the end of your outdoor time, ask partners to show the group the objects they found to be of similar size, larger, and smaller. Encourage children to discuss their predictions and findings with one another.

Observations

- Do children have realistic ideas of how tall they are?
- Which items do children predict will correspond to their height?

Books

Use these books as discussion starters about growth and growing up.

- *Bigger and Smaller* by Robert Proman (Thomas Y. Crowell)
- *Blue Sea* by Robert Kalan (Greenwillow Books)
- *The Growing Story* by Robert Krauss (Harper & Row)

SPIN-OFFS

- Give children plain paper, crayons, and scissors, and ask them to make a traced cutout of one of their feet. Then ask them to look at various objects, and encourage them to measure these items with the cutoffs. Help them record their measurements on a simple picture chart (using tally marks). Later, talk about their recordings.

How Many Blocks Tall?

Children see how they "stack up" by measuring with blocks.

Materials

- unit or 1/2-unit blocks
- large sheet of paper
- rulers
- tape measure

Aim

Children will use observation and problem-solving skills as they measure themselves with blocks.

Warm-Up

Invite a few children to join you, and show them the yard-stick or tape measure. Do any of them recognize these measuring tools? Ask children to think of items they may have measured using these tools. Then demonstrate how they are used by measuring different things in the class-room. Ask children if they can remember the last time they had their heights measured. Do they remember what was used to measure their heights?

Activity

1 Gather children in the art area, and invite them to measure by using the blocks. Begin by deciding which unit blocks you'll use for measurement. Unit or half-unit blocks might work best. Then practice measuring with the blocks by stacking them beside inanimate objects such as chairs or tables.

2 Suggest that children work in pairs to measure each other. Ask the child who's being measured to stand straight and tall while that child's partner builds a tower next to him or her. Have children stop building when the tower is equal to the child's height.

3 Then invite each pair of children to count how many blocks are in the stack. They'll discover how tall their partner is in unit blocks! Now they can trade places and measure the other child.

4 After everyone has had a turn, children can record their block measurements on an experience chart.

Remember

- If it is too hard to build towers as tall as children, have them lie on the floor, and place blocks end-to-end alongside them.

Observations

- In what ways do children record their measurements on the experience chart?

Books

Share these books to enhance children's experiences.

- *Is It Larger, Is It Smaller?* by Tana Hoban (Greenwillow Books)
- *Super, Super, Superwords* by Bruce McMillan (Lothrop, Lee & Shepard)
- *What's That Size?* by Kate Petty (Franklin Watts)

SPIN-OFFS

- After children have had some experience with this, play a game in which they guess how tall someone is in blocks. After they are measured, whose guess comes closest?
- Encourage children to measure other things in the room, such as shelves, table heights, and chairs.

Me and My Shadow

Step outside for a shadow-measuring activity!

Materials

- colored chalk
- yarn or string
- masking tape
- experience-chart paper
- markers or crayons

Aim

Children will use the mathematical skills of nonlinear measurement, estimation, and prediction.

Warm-Up

Gather children outside on a sunny day to look for shadows made by trees, buildings, play structures, furniture, and people. Encourage children to play and experiment with their shadows. They can try to move their bodies to see if their shadows always move with them. As they play, ask them if two people can make their shadows touch without really touching each other. Or ask what happens to their shadows when they turn around.

Activity

1 Pair up children, and ask one child in each pair to trace the other's shadow. Explain that one child needs to stand in the sun on concrete or another hard surface while the other uses chalk to slowly draw a line around the first child's shadow.

2 Help children write their names inside their tracings, and suggest that they exchange roles. Then everyone can stand back and take a look at all the shadows lying about!

3 Now, offer each pair of children a length of yarn or string. Help one child hold the string at the head of the shadow-tracing while the other stretches it to the bottom. Then cut the measured length, and help them measure the other partner's shadow. Ask children if they think their shadows are the same size as they are.

4 Invite each set of partners to test out their predictions by holding the measured portion of string next to the child who was measured. Or the string can be taped to the wall, and children can stand up next to it.

Remember

- Shadows may be longer or shorter, depending on what time of day they were observed.

Observations

- Do children note the difference between the size of their shadows and the size of their bodies?

Books

Here are some fun shadow books to share.

- *Come Out Shadow Wherever You Are!* by Bernice Myers (Scholastic)
- *Shadows* by Tara Gomi (Heian International)

SPIN-OFFS

- Invite children to play a game of shadow tag. In this game, children have to tag one another's shadow instead of one another.
- Invite children to stand so that each child's shadow is touching another child's but the children are not actually touching.

Keeping Your Balance

Make your own pan-balance scale and use it creatively!

Materials

2 of each of the following:

- small plastic bowls or tubs
- scissors
- string
- small sponges
- small stones
- paper napkins
- coat hanger
- pieces of cloth
- washcloths
- pencils

Aim

Children will use the mathematical skills of estimation, prediction, measurement, and recording.

In Advance

Make a pan balance. Use sharp scissors to cut or punch four small holes along the edge of each of the bowls or tubs. (Each set of holes should be across from each other like north, south, east, and west on a map.) Cut eight pieces of string. Tie one string to each hole. Tie the loose ends of the strings so the bowls hang freely from each end of the hanger.

Activity

1 If possible, go out to a playground and demonstrate balance on a seesaw. Invite children to take part in demonstrations that will help them see that when a heavier object or person is placed on one side of the seesaw, it goes down and the other side goes up.

2 Show children the collected pairs of items. Ask them to put one of each pair in the bowls of the pan balance. Ask if the two bowls are hanging on the same level. Ask children to think about why these bowls are at the same level.

3 Now ask children to take one sponge and wet it. Ask them what they think will happen when the wet sponge is placed in one bowl and the dry one in the other. Invite children to test out their predictions. Then encourage children to test out the other sets of items by wetting one item of each pair.

4 End the activity by discussing why some items were made heavier by the water and some were not. Encourage children to try other objects. Keep your pan balance hanging near the math and manipulatives area so children can experiment with weighing other classroom objects.

Observations

- How do children interpret the concepts of *heavy* and *light?*

Books

Here are books that talk about other simple machines.

- *Machines* by Anne Rockwell (Macmillan)
- *The True Book of Toys at Work* by John Lewellen (Children's Press)

SPIN-OFFS

- Place a variety of small classroom items near the pan-balance area, and invite children to use different combinations of objects to balance the scale. Encourage children to record their results.
- Invite children to group objects into two groups — heavy and light. Then ask children to weigh objects against each other to see if these objects remain in their initial categories.

Fill 'er Up!

Together, enjoy this hands-on experience with area and volume.

Materials

- large cardboard cutouts of basic shapes
- masking tape
- unit blocks
- small table-blocks

Aim

Children will use problem-solving, creative-thinking, and fine-motor skills as they make discoveries about volume and area.

Warm-Up

Distribute the cut-out shapes, and invite children to match objects in the room to those shapes. Together, brainstorm a list of objects children may have seen that have the same shape.

Activity

1 Tape a few of the large cut-out cardboard shapes to the floor, and encourage children to cover them completely with different-shaped unit blocks.

2 Tell children the idea of this game is to cover as much of the shape as possible without overlapping any blocks, leaving empty spaces, or letting any blocks hang over the edge. You could say, for example, "It's like doing a puzzle with blocks as your puzzle pieces."

3 When all the shapes are full of unit blocks, talk about differences between the cut-out shapes and the blocks that are needed to fill them in. Ask children which cardboard shape needs the most blocks and which shapes are the most difficult to fill this way. Ask children to think about why this is so.

4 Then put out a set of smaller table blocks and ask children if they think they will need more or less of these smaller blocks to fill in the cardboard cut-out shapes. Suggest that children test their predictions by playing the same game.

Remember

- Encourage children to try to fill the shapes using at least two types of blocks. This allows them to see that an area can be filled in different ways.

Observations

- How do children test their predictions of which shapes need the most or fewest blocks?

Books

Share these shape books at storytime.

- *The Little Circle* by Ann Atwood (Charles Scribner's Sons)
- *Shapes, Shapes, Shapes* by Tana Hoban (Greenwillow Books)
- *Square Is a Shape* by Sharon Lerner (Lerner)

SPIN-OFFS

- Place several boxes of different sizes and shapes in the play area, and invite children to use the bigger unit blocks and then the smaller table blocks to fill the boxes. Ask them which box they think will hold the most blocks. Encourage children to carefully pack each box, rather than randomly throw the blocks in. Suggest that they try to fill each box in a few different ways. Talk about which ways best fill the boxes.

How Much Is There?

Make estimations about volume with raisins and water.

Materials

- plastic containers of various sizes
- chart paper
- crayons and markers
- plastic tub
- measuring cups
- water
- jar of raisins

Aim

Children will use sand, water, and raisins to observe, estimate, experiment with, and evaluate volume.

In Advance

Prepare a chart by drawing pictures of the containers at the top of the chart paper. Underneath each picture, make two columns—one for children's estimations and the other for results. Write children's names down the left side of the chart, and draw lines to make rows.

Activity

1 Explain that an estimation is a guess based on things you see. You can practice estimation with a game of guessing how many raisins are in a jar. Record children's predictions on chart paper, then open the jar and count the number of raisins.

2 Allow time for children to tell whether their guesses are higher or lower than the actual number of raisins. Have fun with the game by eating some of the contents from the jar. Then ask them if there are there more raisins or fewer raisins in the jar than before.

3 Show children the collection of plastic containers, and ask them to pick out which ones they think need the most cups and which ones the fewest cups of water to be completely full. Take turns estimating how many cups of water will fill each container. Help children use tally marks to record their estimations in the appropriate column of the chart.

4 Then help children tally each time a cup of water is added to the container. Compare the estimated amount with the actual measurement. Ask children how close their estimations were. Were they higher or lower than the real number of cups? Encourage children to try different containers.

Observations

- Do children's estimations become more accurate with more practice?

Books

Here are books to share about sand and water.

- *The Quicksand Book* by Tomie dePaola (Holiday House)
- *Sand Cake* by Frank Asch (Crown)
- *The Sun, the Wind, and the Rain* by Lisa Peters (Henry Holt)

SPIN-OFFS

- Prediction is also helpful in building estimation skills. Encourage children to make predictions whenever they can. Before a class trip, invite children to predict what they will see and record their predictions on chart paper. After the trip, revisit the list and compare their predictions with the actual experience.

Experimenting With Time

Help children gain a better understanding of time.

Materials

- various timers (windup kitchen timers, egg timers, sand timers)
- chart paper
- markers

Aim

Children will observe, estimate, and record temporal events.

Warm-Up

Talk with children about time. Discuss how some things, like clocks and timers, show us that time is passing and how we can also see the effect time has on things. Ask children how people would tell time if there were no clocks. Some children may know what time is by events at home or at school. Ask children to share what else helps them tell time.

Activity

1 Present the different timers to the class. Talk about each one, the different ways timers work, and the reasons people use timers. Help children compare the timers. Set two timers to go off in one minute, and see if they both go off at the same time.

2 Help children make time estimations. For example, ask questions such as "How many times can you jump up and down before the sand in this timer runs out?" or "How many plastic-foam balls can you put in a box before the bell rings?" Record children's estimations on a chart, and test them out together.

3 Help children understand that timers can also be used to measure how long it takes to do something. Ask children to choose a timer and measure how long it takes to build a block tower, paint a picture, sing a song, or play a board game. Which activities in your day seem to take the longest? The shortest? Help children list and order a few activities by time.

4 On chart paper, make a graph of how long each activity takes. Encourage children to read the graph to determine which activity took the longest and which took the shortest amount of time.

Observations

- Are children able to work with timers and accurately record the results?

Books

These books can help introduce the concept of time and clocks.

- *All Kinds of Time* by Harry Behn (Harcourt Brace Jovanovich)
- *Clocks* by Tony Barrs (Grossett & Dunlap)
- *Clocks and More Clocks* by Pat Hutchins (Macmillan)
- *It's About Time* by Miriam Schlein (Addison-Wesley)

SPIN-OFFS

- Make a group sand-timer. In a glass jar, suspend a paper cup with a hole in the bottom. Tape the rim of the paper cup to the rim of the jar and add sand to the cup. Children can observe the timer and watch time pass in a concrete way as the sand piles up in the jar. Ask children what would happen if more holes were in the cup. Test children's ideas. Use a timer to help you place enough sand in the cup to make it last exactly one minute, two minutes, or three minutes, and so on.

Circle Crayons

Recycle old crayons!

Materials

- muffin tins
- paper cupcake liners
- old, broken crayons (with paper removed)
- experience-chart paper
- drawing paper
- potholders
- oven

Aim

Children will experience the properties of temperature as they observe the melting process of crayons.

In Advance

Encourage children to save small pieces of broken crayons at home and at school. A day or two before this activity, collect crayon pieces into one or two large containers, and invite children to help remove any paper coatings.

Activity

1 Gather three or four children around a craft table equipped with muffin tins, paper liners, and crayon pieces. Help children place a paper liner into each compartment of the muffin tin.

2 Next, invite them to put several crayons in each compartment. Some may want to separate colors while others may prefer to mix them. Encourage them to fill all the compartments until each is approximately a quarter- to half-full.

3 Ask children what they think will happen to the crayons when they are heated, and record their predictions on an experience chart. Put the tins in the oven at 350 degrees for about 10 minutes. Then remove and set until cool. If possible, remove the muffin tins from the oven every three minutes during the melting process. Talk about how the crayons look at each stage of the heating and cooling, and refer back to children's predictions.

4 Now pass out drawing paper and invite children to experiment with their "new" circle crayons!

Remember

- Many paper cupcake liners have zigzag edges. To give crayons a smoother edge, try pressing the liners gently between your thumb and forefinger before you help children place them in the tins.

Observations

- How did children's predictions match the outcome of the heating and cooling process?

Books

Share these books about shapes with children.

- *Round and Square* by J. Martin (The Platt & Munk Co.)
- *Shapes* by M. Schlein (William R. Scott)
- *Shapes and Things* by Tana Hoban (Macmillan)

SPIN-OFFS

- Use a cookie sheet lined with waxed paper on which children can place crayon pieces in specific patterns or shapes. Encourage children to guess what the shapes will look like after the crayons have been heated and cooled. Then heat and melt the crayons again, showing children how heat continues to change the shapes.

Indoor/Outdoor Plants

On your mark, get set, grow!

Materials

- 2 plant markers per child
- 2 small planter pots per child
- fast-growing seeds
- markers
- fork
- popsicle sticks
- magnifiers
- soil
- spade
- watering can
- oaktag paper

Aim

Children will measure and record the growth of plants from seeds.

In Advance

Schedule a 15-minute period at the same time of day for several weeks for children to measure and record plant growth. Label plant markers with children's names.

Warm-Up

Open a discussion about what makes plants grow. Talk about which kinds of plants can grow indoors or outdoors.

Activity

1 Distribute seeds, markers, and pots. Invite children to use magnifiers to examine the seeds closely.

2 Using the spade and fork, help children fill the pots with soil and plant the seeds. Ask them to place some pots inside near a window and some outside in an area that receives both sun and shade. Then ask them to water both sets of pots. Invite children to predict which seeds will grow faster.

3 Encourage children to check the pots every day for signs of growth. Help them add water if the soil is too dry. When the seedlings start to grow, ask children to mark the plants' heights on the popsicle sticks. Use a different stick every day for each plant.

4 Give each child a piece of oaktag paper. Help them chart their plants' growth by pasting the popsicle sticks on the oaktag paper under columns marked "Indoor" and "Outdoor." After a few weeks, gather children and ask which plants grew faster, the indoor ones or the outdoor ones.

Remember

- Choose seeds that will grow quickly, such as lima beans or carrots.

Observations

- What ideas do children have about why plants grow differently inside and outside?

Books

These books will inspire your young gardeners.

- *The Carrot Seed* by Ruth Krauss (Harper & Row)
- *Grow It for Fun* by Denny A. Robson (Franklin Watts)
- *How Do Things Grow?* by Althea (Troll)

SPIN-OFFS

- Create a special garden in which children are encouraged to plant anything they think might grow. Children may choose apple seeds, vegetable roots—even orange peels! Place markers in the soil to show what has been planted. Invite children to observe their garden's progress. Then note a chart showing what grew and what didn't.

A Measuring Treasure Hunt

Children can find lots to measure right in their classroom!

Materials

- construction or newsprint paper
- brightly colored yarn
- yardstick
- ruler
- crayons
- markers
- tape

In Advance

Cut yarn into pieces of varying length from 2–18 inches.

Warm-Up

Talk with children about measurement. Show them a ruler or yardstick to demonstrate the usual way people measure things. Then introduce the yarn pieces as an alternative method of measuring.

Activity

1 Show the pieces of yarn to the groups and ask each child to choose a piece to use on a measuring "treasure hunt." Ask children to look around the room to find one thing that is the same size as their piece of yarn.

2 Demonstrate how to use the yarn for measuring by choosing a piece of yarn and inviting children to follow you around the room as you hold your yarn up to different items. Help children see and understand how to measure and how to check if the yarn and the object are the same length.

3 Now encourage children to search the room to find objects the same length as their yarn segments. Enjoy the excitement as children find objects that match!

4 Now ask children to trade their piece of yarn for one of a different length. First, invite them to measure items that matched their previous yarn-length. How does it compare? Then encourage children to find objects that match their new yarn-lengths.

Remember

- As an extension, consider asking children to compare lengths of yarn. Then help them arrange the pieces of yarn in order of length. This will give them practice in order and seriation.

Observations

- Do children use yarn only to measure length, or do they measure around items too?

Books

Increase children's understanding of measurement with these delightful stories.

- *Big and Little, Up and Down* by Ethel Berkley (Addison-Wesley)
- *Inch by Inch* Leo Lionni (Astor-Honor)
- *One Step Two* by Charlotte Zolotow (Lothrop, Lee & Shepard)

SPIN-OFFS

- Record children's measurement findings on long sheets of paper laid sideways. Each time one takes a measurement, tape the child's piece of yarn across the paper, write his or her name, and write or draw a picture of the "matching" object. Then encourage the child to pick out a new piece of yarn and look again. Take time to look at the chart together.

Activity Plans for Geometry

Rectangles, triangles, circles, and squares — children know that shapes are everywhere! From an early age, children learn to recognize things by shape. A pizza pie is a circle, but when it's sliced it's a triangle! First, children recognize basic flat shapes, and then they grow to identify three-dimensional shapes. Block building is just one example of children's natural interest in geometric concepts. Concrete experiences with both two- and three-dimensional shapes will lay the foundation for a lifetime of geometry.

Blocks provide meaningful experiences with spatial relationships.

Throughout the Day

- Invite children to participate in a "Shape of the Day" game. Search for as many of the same-shaped items as you can throughout the day. Encourage children to notice all of the different sizes and colors that shapes can come in.
- Invite children to point out objects with unusual shapes, and ask them to create shape names for these objects. For example, a stuffed animal may be "teddy bear shaped."
- Allow children time throughout the day to explore the spaces around them, indoors and outdoors. Ask children to describe their favorite space and why it's their favorite.

Around the Room

- Set out a variety of maps and mazes for children to explore. You may even suggest that children make a three-dimensional map or maze in a play area within your classroom.
- Cut out a variety of basic shapes in different colors. Place them all in a box, and encourage children to label objects in the classroom with the same shape and color cutout. For example, they may tape a red circle to the playground ball.

Shapes in Our Room

We see shapes everywhere!

Materials

- oaktag cutouts of shapes
- experience-chart paper
- construction paper
- scissors
- crayons
- markers
- glue

Aim

Children will learn about the classroom as they problem-solve with shapes.

Warm-Up

Gather children and brainstorm a list of different shapes they see in the world. When as they think of a shape, discuss things that have that shape. For example, a circle is the shape of a clock, a wheel, and a doughnut. Write down all the shapes they mention.

Activity

1 After providing construction paper and scissors, invite children to cut out several shapes to match the shapes they discussed. You may want to provide the oaktag patterns for children to trace and cut out.

2 Then ask children to choose a shape to find in the classroom. Allow them to use their cut-out shapes as guides for finding shapes in the classroom. Encourage children to work in pairs to find as many objects of that particular shape as they can.

3 Gather children and record their findings on an experience chart. You might use "Our Classroom Shapes Graph" as a title. Discuss which shape was found most often.

4 Let children each pick several of the precut shapes, and provide them with sheets of paper and glue. Invite them to create real world scenes, pictures, or designs by gluing the shapes on the paper and adding their own illustrations with crayons or markers.

Remember

- Reinforce shape and classroom vocabulary by making encouraging comments, such as "I see you found five circles in the science area."

Observations

- Do children see several different shapes combined in some objects? Do they recognize the difference between similar shapes, such as an oval and a circle?

Books

These shape books may inspire your budding artists.

- *The Little Circle* by Ann Atwood (Charles Scribner's Sons)
- *The Parade of Shapes* by Sylvia Tester (Child's World)
- *Shapes and Things* by Tana Hoban (Macmillan)

SPIN-OFFS

- Invite children to create a "Playground Shapes" graph. Encourage them to record the different shapes they see in things like slides, swings, balls, and buckets.
- Provide children with blocks and different-shaped recyclable materials, and ask them to create three-dimensional sculptures. Encourage children to examine the materials to find the shapes they want to use.

Twister Fun!

Try this fun and interactive math game.

Materials

- 3' x 5' sheet of butcher paper
- various sheets of colored paper
- scissors
- dark marker
- box or basket
- masking tape

Aim

Children will use gross-motor skills as they interact to identify squares, circles, and triangles.

In Advance

Make a game board by dividing butcher paper into three columns lengthwise and five rows across. From the colored paper, cut triangles, circles, and squares to fit inside the squares on the butcher paper. Also cut small shapes that match (in color) the larger ones and place them in the box or basket. Securely tape the larger colored shapes in the squares on the game board and tape the game board to the floor.

Activity

1 Gather children together and divide them into groups of three or four by distributing a small cut-out shape to each child. Invite all the "circles" to stand together as a group, all the "squares" to stand together, and so on.

2 Invite one group at a time to stand near the edges of the paper. Choose one child to go first, and help that child choose one of the shapes from the basket. Invite that child to say what he or she picked—"red square" for example.

3 Together, find a red square and ask the child to put his hand or foot on that square. Give the other children turns so that everyone playing is touching a space on the board.

4 Next, choose another shape for children, explaining that they need to move a different part of their bodies to touch the second shape. Continue playing as long as children are interested, and then let another group play.

Remember

- As children become more familiar with the game, allow them to think of variations and to help pick shapes from the basket.

Observations

- Are children able to locate both color and shape on the game board?

Books

These books about shapes and colors will be fun to share.

- *Colors* by Gwenda Turner (Viking Kestral)
- *Shapes and Things* by Tana Hoban (Macmillan)
- *Tom's Rainbow Walk* by Catherine Anholt (Little, Brown)

SPIN-OFFS

- Invite children to draw from the box again, and chart all of the different color and shape combinations they notice.
- Using this chart, ask children to explore the classroom to look for objects that would fit these color-shape combinations.

Puzzling Shapes

It's fun to turn block shapes into towers!

Materials

- masking tape (preferably in different colors)
- several large sheets of butcher paper
- markers or crayons
- blocks

Aim

Children will use blocks to explore the math concepts of shape, area, perimeter, and graphing.

In Advance

Draw six or seven shape outlines on large paper placed on the floor in the block area. Include a circle, a triangle, and a square, as well as less familiar shapes, such as hexagons and ovals. Place blocks of different sizes and shapes on the floor to create one large shape. Use tape to trace around each block. Then remove the blocks. You've created a "floor puzzle" for children to fill in.

Activity

1 Assign each child a different-shaped block. Ask children how many of their blocks they think will fit into the shapes on the floor. Let children explore the shapes you drew on the paper by filling them with blocks of the same type. Encourage them to build a tower using all the blocks from inside one shape.

2 Now try some graphing. Draw a straight line on the butcher paper, and invite each child to line up his or her blocks along it. Help children trace their line of blocks with a marker, and label each line with a shape and a name. Then let children remove the blocks and see which line is longer. Ask them to think about why.

3 Explore the concept of perimeter by inviting children to make a line of blocks around the edge of each large shape. Ask children to count the blocks in their line.

4 Finally, encourage children to solve the block floor puzzle you made. Watch them discover which blocks will fit within the lines.

Remember

- Reinforce shape vocabulary throughout this activity by using words like *hexagon*, *pentagon*, and *oval.*

Observations

- What problem-solving skills do children use? How do children interpret the graph?

Books

With the help of these books, your class will have lots of shape fun!

- *Brian Wildsmith's 1, 2, 3*, by Brian Wildsmith (Millbrook Press)
- *Shapes* by Jon. J. Reiss (Bradbury Press)
- *Spirals, Curves, Fanshapes, and Lines* by Tana Hoban (Greenwillow Books)

SPIN-OFFS

- Invite all the children together to fill in the space around the shapes with blocks, leaving the inside of the shapes empty. Ask them to guess how many blocks they have used.
- Invite children to make graphs for perimeters and areas of the same shape. Ask children to graph the number of blocks used for measuring each, and encourage them to think about why one has more.

A Room Just for Me

Now children can build the rooms of their dreams—with blocks!

Materials

- assorted props (such as pillows and picture frames)
- large, hollow cardboard blocks
- planks and boards
- construction paper
- wallpaper samples
- floor tiles
- unit blocks
- rug remnants
- sleeping bags
- blankets
- boxes

Aim

Children will gain experience with structure and spatial relationships as they design an ideal room.

Activity

1 Show children some of the props, and encourage them to think of what their dream room would look like. How tall will it be? How wide? Will it have a door? Then invite them to select the blocks they need to build a room of their own.

2 Allow children to construct on their own for a while. Then comment from time to time with your own observations, offering assistance when needed. Encourage them to use the blocks and boxes to build furniture and other things they want for their rooms.

3 Then introduce new props as children's constructions near completion. To add to their rooms, they can also construct appliances or other props in the woodworking area.

4 When children's rooms are done, bring the other children in your group together, and allow the builders to talk about the rooms and furnishings. Ask them questions about their rooms, and encourage the other children to do so as well.

Remember

- If space in your classroom is limited, this activity can be adapted by having children work in small groups.

Observations

- In what ways do children plan out their rooms before they begin building?

Books

Here are some books to share with children in their special "rooms."

- *Block City* by Robert Louis Stevenson (Dutton)
- *A Chair for My Mother* by Vera B. Williams (Greenwillow Books)
- *The Lost and Found House* by Consuelo Joerns (Four Winds)

SPIN-OFFS

- Take pictures or ask children to draw pictures of their newly created rooms. Then invite them to write or dictate captions for the pictures for display or even to be made into a book.
- Invite children to use boxes as structures and to create rooms inside them. Encourage children to use boxes side-by-side or on top of each other for varying effects.

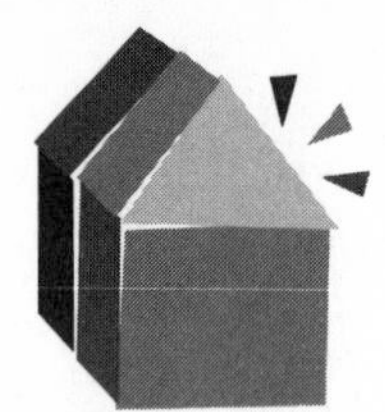

From Blocks to Buildings

Children use the same blocks to build many different buildings.

Materials

- matching unit blocks or table blocks of various sizes and shapes

Aim

Children will use observation, comparison, and perceptual skills as they make and compare their constructions.

Warm-Up

Discuss the concepts of *same* and *different*, using classroom objects to demonstrate the concepts. Play a matching game in which children match objects that are the same.

Activity

1 Move to the block area, and ask children to help you assemble two sets of blocks that are the same. This is a good matching activity to help them understand the concept of *same*. As children find the matching blocks, ask them to sort the blocks into separate piles.

2 Before they begin, divide children into pairs and ask them to build a wall between them by propping up books. You can also use a low divider or screen.

3 Explain to children that both sets of blocks are the same. Then ask if they think that their buildings will look alike. Encourage them to build their buildings any way they want, without looking at those of their friends.

4 When each pair is finished, remove the wall or divider so they can see each other's buildings. Ask how each building is different from the other. Are there things that are the same about them? Suggest that children walk around the buildings to examine all sides. Which is the longest? The highest?

Remember

- Children may not be able to see the differences in their structures right away. You may need to help them verbalize the differences by pointing out a few at first.

Observations

- Were children able to work on their structures independently, without looking at their partner's? How do children describe the differences in each other's block buildings?

Books

Include these books about differences in your classroom library.

- *Becca Backward, Becca Frontward* by Bruce McMillan (Lothrop, Lee & Shepard)
- *Bigger and Smaller* by Robert Froman (Thomas Y. Crowell)
- *Super, Super, Superwords* by Bruce McMillan (Lothrop, Lee & Shepard)

SPIN-OFFS

- The concepts of *same* and *different* can also be explored through art. For example, two children may draw a picture using identical sheets of paper and sets of crayons or make collages with paper scraps of the same shape, size, and color. How do the final products differ?

Neighborhood Maps

Children create a little corner of their neighborhood.

Materials

- masking tape (preferably in different colors)
- unit or table blocks
- junk material (such as egg cartons, tubes, small boxes, and containers)
- experience-chart paper
- construction paper
- local map (optional)
- markers

Aim

Children will use creative-thinking, problem-solving, and spatial-awareness skills as they cooperate in the construction of a neighborhood map.

Warm-Up

Walk together around the neighborhood. Look carefully at buildings and important roads nearby. When you return, record children's observations on an experience chart.

Activity

1 Talk about maps and, if possible, locate where your street or building is on a local map. Then explain that you're going to make your own neighborhood map out of blocks and other things.

2 Provide construction paper and tape, and help children construct a "floor" of your map. Use tape to make the roads, and green paper for yards and parks.

3 Next, talk about what buildings to include and discuss where on the map these buildings should be placed.

4 Encourage children to work in pairs or small groups to build a variety of structures they see in their neighborhood. It may be best to start with your school building and then move to buildings farther away.

Remember

- If possible, take photographs of the buildings and significant landmarks you see on your walk. Add these to the experience chart, and encourage children to refer to them as they work.

Observations

- Do children have specific ideas of what should be included on their maps?

Books

Share these interesting books about neighborhoods with your class.

- *All Kinds of Signs* by Seymore Reit (Western)
- *The House With the Red Roof* by William Wise (Putnam Publishing Group)
- *The Little House* by Virginia Burton (Houghton Mifflin)
- *What is a Community?* by Caroline Arnold (Watts)

SPIN-OFFS

- Distribute large sheets of drawing paper and crayons to children, and invite them to draw a map of their route to school. Encourage them to include any special landmarks or points of interest they see on their way.
- Children may also explore mapping individually by creating maps of their homes. Encourage children to label where family members sleep, eat, work, and play.

Over, Under, and Around

Children may enjoy building around these obstacles.

Materials

- 3–6 large, hollow cardboard blocks
- large cardboard carton
- unit blocks
- small table
- chair
- low divider

Aim

Children will use problem-solving skills as they build around different obstacles with blocks.

In Advance

Cut the top and bottom off the large carton. Then place it and the other materials in the block area so that children have room to build around, over, through, and under them.

Warm-Up

Set up a mini obstacle course using some objects in your room. Explain that to get through the course, you have to go over, under, around, and through the objects in your path. Let children practice going through this mini-course.

Activity

1 Show children the obstacles in the block area. Allow them sufficient time to examine the course and ask questions such as "Which ones can you build through? Which ones can you build over?"

2 Invite children to build in pairs or small groups. Encourage them to talk to one another as they work, sharing their ideas.

3 Children can experiment with different ways to build with or around the obstacles. After they have used one method, encourage them to try another.

4 Give children time to talk about their constructions. Encourage them to describe how they used the obstacles in their constructions. Listen for descriptive words such as *over, under, around,* and *through.*

Remember

- This activity can be simplified by using only one concept each day. For example, set up several objects for children to build *over* on one day and *under* the next day.

Observations

- Did children find that certain obstacles were easier to work with than others? Which ones? Why?

Books

Here are some books to share after the activity.

- *Over, Under & Through* by Tana Hoban (Macmillan)
- *We're Going on a Bear Hunt* by Michael Rosen (McElderry)
- *Where Is My Friend?* by Betsy Maestro (Crown)

SPIN-OFFS

- Invite children to construct their own block obstacle courses. Encourage them to explain the obstacles they set up and talk about the challenges they create. Children may want to build courses to use themselves or to challenge their friends.

Picture Surprise

Children explore symmetry through painting and folding.

- finger paint in 2 or 3 different colors
- 2–3 small bowls
- 2–3 plastic spoons (teaspoon or smaller)
- finger-paint paper
- newspaper

Aim

Children will discover the concept of *symmetry* by using finger paints.

In Advance

Cover the art table with newspaper. Then put a small amount of paint and a spoon in each bowl, and place them on the table along with finger-paint paper.

Activity

1 Gather children around the table, and offer each a sheet of finger-paint paper. Explain that they will be painting in a special way. When they finish, there will be a surprise.

2 Ask children to fold their papers in half, shiny side in, and open them again. Then invite them to use spoons to place their paint dabs. Help children to fold their papers in half again. Encourage children to rub their hands over their folded papers. As children rub, encourage discussion by asking them what is happening to the paint and what they think their pictures will look like.

3 Ask children to open up their papers, and encourage them to talk about what they see. You can extend their discussion by asking if their pictures look the same on both sides. How do they think their pictures got that way? You may want to introduce the word *symmetry.* Invite children to make more symmetrical finger paintings.

4 Invite children to put their pictures together in a book. Children can then examine and discuss the pictures over time, helping them to develop an understanding of symmetry.

Remember

- This is not a formal lesson in symmetry. Instead, it's an opportunity for children to discover and experience this concept on their own.

Observations

- Do children notice on their own that pictures look the same on both sides?

Books

These books feature lots of interesting designs.

- *It Looked Like Spilt Milk* by Charles B. Shaw (Harper & Row)
- *Look Twice!* by Duncan Birmingham (Tarquin)
- *Shadows and Reflections* by Tana Hoban (Greenwillow Books)

SPIN-OFFS

- Invite children to look through old magazines or catalogs, and encourage them to draw a line down the middle of pictures they think might be symmetrical. Talk about the pictures together. Are the images exactly the same on each side?

Neighborhood Maps

Children create a little corner of their neighborhood.

Materials

- masking tape (preferably in different colors)
- unit or table blocks
- junk material (such as egg cartons, tubes, small boxes, and containers)
- experience-chart paper
- construction paper
- local map (optional)
- markers

Aim

Children will use creative-thinking, problem-solving, and spatial-awareness skills as they cooperate in the construction of a neighborhood map.

Warm-Up

Walk together around the neighborhood. Look carefully at buildings and important roads nearby. When you return, record children's observations on an experience chart.

Activity

1 Talk about maps and, if possible, locate where your street or building is on a local map. Then explain that you're going to make your own neighborhood map out of blocks and other things.

2 Provide construction paper and tape, and help children construct a "floor" of your map. Use tape to make the roads, and green paper for yards and parks.

3 Next, talk about what buildings to include and discuss where on the map these buildings should be placed.

4 Encourage children to work in pairs or small groups to build a variety of structures they see in their neighborhood. It may be best to start with your school building and then move to buildings farther away.

Remember

- If possible, take photographs of the buildings and significant landmarks you see on your walk. Add these to the experience chart, and encourage children to refer to them as they work.

Observations

- Do children have specific ideas of what should be included on their maps?

Books

Share these interesting books about neighborhoods with your class.

- *All Kinds of Signs* by Seymore Reit (Western)
- *The House With the Red Roof* by William Wise (Putnam Publishing Group)
- *The Little House* by Virginia Burton (Houghton Mifflin)
- *What is a Community?* by Caroline Arnold (Watts)

SPIN-OFFS

- Distribute large sheets of drawing paper and crayons to children, and invite them to draw a map of their route to school. Encourage them to include any special landmarks or points of interest they see on their way.
- Children may also explore mapping individually by creating maps of their homes. Encourage children to label where family members sleep, eat, work, and play.

Over, Under, and Around

Children may enjoy building around these obstacles.

Materials

- 3–6 large, hollow cardboard blocks
- large cardboard carton
- unit blocks
- chair
- small table
- low divider

Aim

Children will use problem-solving skills as they build around different obstacles with blocks.

In Advance

Cut the top and bottom off the large carton. Then place it and the other materials in the block area so that children have room to build around, over, through, and under them.

Warm-Up

Set up a mini obstacle course using some objects in your room. Explain that to get through the course, you have to go over, under, around, and through the objects in your path. Let children practice going through this mini-course.

Activity

1 Show children the obstacles in the block area. Allow them sufficient time to examine the course and ask questions such as "Which ones can you build through? Which ones can you build over?"

2 Invite children to build in pairs or small groups. Encourage them to talk to one another as they work, sharing their ideas.

3 Children can experiment with different ways to build with or around the obstacles. After they have used one method, encourage them to try another.

4 Give children time to talk about their constructions. Encourage them to describe how they used the obstacles in their constructions. Listen for descriptive words such as *over, under, around,* and *through.*

Remember

- This activity can be simplified by using only one concept each day. For example, set up several objects for children to build *over* on one day and *under* the next day.

Observations

- Did children find that certain obstacles were easier to work with than others? Which ones? Why?

Books

Here are some books to share after the activity.

- *Over, Under & Through* by Tana Hoban (Macmillan)
- *We're Going on a Bear Hunt* by Michael Rosen (McElderry)
- *Where Is My Friend?* by Betsy Maestro (Crown)

SPIN-OFFS

- Invite children to construct their own block obstacle courses. Encourage them to explain the obstacles they set up and talk about the challenges they create. Children may want to build courses to use themselves or to challenge their friends.

Picture Surprise

Children explore symmetry through painting and folding.

- finger paint in 2 or 3 different colors
- 2–3 small bowls
- 2–3 plastic spoons (teaspoon or smaller)
- finger-paint paper
- newspaper

Aim

Children will discover the concept of *symmetry* by using finger paints.

In Advance

Cover the art table with newspaper. Then put a small amount of paint and a spoon in each bowl, and place them on the table along with finger-paint paper.

Activity

1 Gather children around the table, and offer each a sheet of finger-paint paper. Explain that they will be painting in a special way. When they finish, there will be a surprise.

2 Ask children to fold their papers in half, shiny side in, and open them again. Then invite them to use spoons to place their paint dabs. Help children to fold their papers in half again. Encourage children to rub their hands over their folded papers. As children rub, encourage discussion by asking them what is happening to the paint and what they think their pictures will look like.

3 Ask children to open up their papers, and encourage them to talk about what they see. You can extend their discussion by asking if their pictures look the same on both sides. How do they think their pictures got that way? You may want to introduce the word *symmetry*. Invite children to make more symmetrical finger paintings.

4 Invite children to put their pictures together in a book. Children can then examine and discuss the pictures over time, helping them to develop an understanding of symmetry.

Remember

- This is not a formal lesson in symmetry. Instead, it's an opportunity for children to discover and experience this concept on their own.

Observations

- Do children notice on their own that pictures look the same on both sides?

Books

These books feature lots of interesting designs.

- *It Looked Like Spilt Milk* by Charles B. Shaw (Harper & Row)
- *Look Twice!* by Duncan Birmingham (Tarquin)
- *Shadows and Reflections* by Tana Hoban (Greenwillow Books)

SPIN-OFFS

- Invite children to look through old magazines or catalogs, and encourage them to draw a line down the middle of pictures they think might be symmetrical. Talk about the pictures together. Are the images exactly the same on each side?